A DAY TO REMEMBER

A LIFETIME TO FORGET

J. RENEE

Hᴏᴛ ᴛᴇᴀʀs ᴘᴏᴜʀᴇᴅ ᴅᴏᴡɴ ᴍʏ ʙᴜʀɴɪɴɢ ᴄʜᴇᴇᴋs. I ᴛʀɪᴇᴅ ᴛᴏ blink them away before they fell but the stinging with each slap to the face was unbearable. Time seemed to be moving in slow motion and I just wanted to get this over with. This was a daily thing, me getting slapped by my stepsisters. At twenty years old I was still too weak to fight back. Even if it wasn't four against one I would always lose. She smacked me again and this time my glasses flew off my face and onto the floor. This time I didn't stop the tears from flowing. Crying always made it worse so I tried not to do it but Christiana was six slaps in and the stinging only grew more intense.

"Chrissy leave that girl alone. You know she's weak." My stepmother said walking into the kitchen.

"But mom she's disrespectful and you always taught us not to let anybody disrespect us."

"True but you know Sparkle isn't like you guys. You're my children which means you're strong. Sparkle on the other hand is." She said tapping her hand against her chin." Well, she's ugly and weak. We all know she'll never amount to anything so just leave her alone. I'm pretty sure she still has shit to do."

My stepmother grabbed the breakfast sandwich I made off the table and walked out the door. She was probably on her way to meet up with one of the many men she slept with. Cuz we all knew her ass aint have a job. It didn't matter how many times I told my father about her cheating he didn't believe me. After a while, I just stopped telling him. Ever since he married Angela my life had gone to shit and with him overseas I had nobody.

"Hurry up and make my plate," Christiana demanded.

Rushing back to the stove I fixed her the breakfast I had made. Christiana snatched the plate out of my hand and rolled her eyes at me. The twins Asia and Ava grabbed a plate and I piled on the food. They followed behind her like the sad little puppies they were. Once they were gone I finally breathed. Picking up my glasses off the floor I inspected them. Thank god they weren't broken. Angela told me since I kept asking to be smacked she wouldn't get me another pair. I had no money so I couldn't do it myself. Walking over to the sink I grabbed a paper towel and wet it with cold water before dabbing my eyes with it. I had to go out soon and didn't want puffy eyes. I got myself together quickly and made me a plate for later. I needed to hurry up and clean the kitchen so I could go pick up their dry cleaning. I had a long day ahead of me and it was only ten am. As I cleaned I sung quietly to myself. I loved singing but it wasn't allowed in the house, at least from me anyway. They always told me I had a horrible voice and that I sounded like a cat in heat. This was the one thing my mom and I had in common and since she went to prison I held this close to my heart.

I washed all the dishes and as I put the rag up Christiana came back in with all their dirty dishes. Dumping them into the sink she laughed and disappeared back into the living room. Sighing I turned the water back on so I could finish. These dirty bitches kept so many dishes in their rooms it was ridiculous. My hands were wrinkled and starting to get numb from all the scrubbing I had just done. I quickly washed the dishes and went upstairs to my room. This was my sanctuary. It wasn't much but it was mine. I sat on my bed and picked up the picture of my mom that I kept on the dresser. Some days I was so embarrassed I would come to my room and place my mother's picture face down. I didn't want her to see me like this. She would be so disappointed in me if she knew what was happening. It had been almost ten years since she has been gone and I missed her every day. Most days I wished it was me that was in prison. Instead, I was living in this hell with no way out. I wanted a job but Angela made it clear the only job I would ever have was being their maid. Placing my mother's picture back on the dresser I pulled out something to wear for the day. I didn't have many choices but I decided on a pair of black jeans and a baby blue sweater I knitted myself for winter with some black converses. I checked myself in the mirror and realized I had a rip on the seam of my thigh. Taking off the pants off I quickly sewed up the rip. I would have to ask Angela for some new pants, these wouldn't be able to last much longer. After I sewed it up I put the pants back on and got ready to go. Angela was nice enough to get me a metro card to travel around with and the next bus came in ten minutes so I needed to hurry. I grabbed the small purse I knitted and put my house keys in it along with my metro card. I made sure to grab the laundry ticket Angela gave me this morning I didn't want to have any problems tonight. I quickly brushed my fro into a puff and was ready to go. As I walked out the door I ran straight into Asia.

"I'm so sorry."

"It's cool Spark. Where you off too?"

"Pick up the laundry and a few other errands," I replied.

"Okay be safe."

"Asia, what are you doing?" Christiana barked from her bedroom door.

"Making sure ugly here doesn't forget our stuff." She replied rolling her eyes at me.

"Oh okay, well Sparkle hurry I need my medicine," Christiana said slamming the door behind her.

Asia didn't say anything else she just walked back to her room. Asia was always nice to me when nobody else was around but soon as Christiana came she started acting like a bitch again. I hated that fake shit but it felt good to have someone to talk to sometimes. I hurried down the stairs and walked to the bus stop. The weather was still a little tricky, some days it was warm and some days it was freezing. Luckily today was more on the warmer side. It wasn't too cold which I was thankful for. This thin ass coat probably couldn't make it through a brutal winter. I made it to the bus stop just as the bus pulled up. I got on and sat in the back. Staring out the window I took in the beauty of Fall in NY. New York was beautiful all year round but it was something about Fall in New York I loved. From the smell in the air to my favorite fall snack, caramel apples. It made my heart smile. Lost in my thoughts I almost missed my stop. I pulled the stop cord and made my way to the door. Getting off the bus I walked straight into the cleaners.

"Hey, Jim." I greeted.

"Sparkle! My favorite customer." He smiled." How are you today?"

"I'm okay Jim, hanging in there. How are you? How's the family?"

"Everyone is good Spark. Jane will be home next weekend. She asks about you all the time."

"Aww tell her I said hi, I'll make sure to stop by next week to see her."

"I will so what can I do for you today?"

Passing Jim my tickets I sat down while he disappeared through the back. Staring out the window I let myself get lost in my thoughts again. I tended to space out a lot, it kept me sane. With everything going on in my life my mind was the only place I could escape to. There were still so many things I had to do today. I still needed to go to the Pharmacy once I got back around the way and then go grocery shopping. Plus I had to make dinner for everyone and I still had no idea what I was going to make.

"Excuse me is someone sitting here?" I heard.

Shaking my thoughts away I looked up to find the prettiest cognac colored eyes staring back at me. My heart began to stammer in my chest. When he smiled at me I blinked twice to make sure I wasn't dreaming.

"Uhh no, here you go," I replied moving my purse.

When he sat down I got a strong whiff of his cologne. He smelled so good I found myself drooling. I had never seen a man this fine before. He was tall chocolate and handsome. His chiseled face had two deep dimples on each side. When he licked his juicy lips time stopped. I could only imagine what they would feel like against mine. I never kissed before but I wouldn't mind kissing him. In the books I read, they always described kissing as knee buckling. I couldn't wait to experience that.

"Miss you don't have to stare" he chuckled.

"Oh! My! God!" I gasped." I'm so sorry."

All the blood in my body rushed to my cheeks. This was so embarrassing. He probably thought I was weird and I couldn't blame him. Get it together Sparkle I said to myself.

"Its cool little mama." He smiled showing off his perfect teeth.

Just then Jim came back. I held on to my purse and scurried over to Jim. I needed to get out of here I couldn't believe I just did that. What the hell is wrong with me?

"Here you go." He said passing me the clothes.

"Wait Jim this is only three of the items. I had four."

"I know but the other one isn't ready. It had a huge stain when it came to me and it's not coming out. I'm working on it, I should be done by tomorrow hopefully."

"Oh no." I sighed." What am I going to do?"

"I promise I'll have it, don't be sad." He said gently touching my hand.

I just knew if I didn't bring everything back I would be in big trouble. Who knows what kinds of cruel punishment she would have for me. Last time she made me wash all of their dirty ass clothes by hand. Which wouldn't have been so bad if it wasn't months of dirty clothes.

"Are you okay?" Jim asked.

"No, but it's nothing I can do about it." I pouted.

"I'm sorry." Jim apologized.

"It's not your fault Jim, I'll deal with the consequences."

"It's not that deep little mama don't be sad." The man added trying to cheer me up.

I looked over at him and he smiled causing my insides to get warm. In the back of my mind though I knew it was that deep. At least to Angela and the girls. I tried to stay out of their way as much as possible but even when I was in my room not bothering anyone they still found something to bitch about.

"I wish it was that simple," I replied.

Turning my attention back to Jim I thanked him. I grabbed my stuff and headed out the door. Before I left I made sure to get one last look. I knew I could never get a man like him. At least I had someone to daydream about later. Soon as I stepped outside the bus was pulling off. I tried to flag him down but he kept going.

"Fuck." I cursed.

"Seems like you're having a rough day," I heard from behind.

His deep raspy voice sent chills down my spine. So much so that I was afraid to turn around.

"You can say that again," I mumbled.

"What did you say?"

He was much taller than I was, I could feel him hovering over me as he stood there. It was making me nervous. Usually, when people stood this close it was because they were going to hit me or scream in my face. I hated people in my personal space I couldn't breathe when they were that close. Unfortunately, the bitches knew that and always got up in my face.

"I-I said you can say that again," I stuttered.

"When you talk to people you should look up at them and not at the ground. We can't hear you little mama."

"Sorry," I mumbled.

"Stop apologizing it's aight," He said moving from behind me.

"I'm sorry I can't help it."

I wanted to look into his beautiful eyes but I was afraid. I didn't remember the last time I had an interaction with a man besides Jim and the man at the pharmacy. Most men found me repulsive, at least the ones the girls brought to the house. I didn't think I was that ugly but then again, I never had a boyfriend before so maybe I was.

"Little mama do you hear me?" He asked.

"Huh? I'm sorry did you say something?" I replied finally looking at him.

He chuckled and smiled at me. Looking at him his eyes seemed to pierce through my soul. It was like he could see me and not see through me like everyone else.

"Focus baby girl. I asked you did you want a ride."

"Oh umm, no thanks. I don't want to be a nuisance."

"It's no problem, I have time. Plus, I won't take no for an answer."

Leaving me standing there he walked away towards his car. When he stopped at a black BMW I began to wonder what he did. I was able to finally get a good look at him. He wore a black polo sweat suit with some black and red sneakers. I could tell he worked out faithfully. I just wanted to wrap myself in his big arms while laying on his chest. This probably wasn't a good idea getting in a car with some strange man but at this point in my life, I hoped someone would kidnap my ass. That would probably be my only chance to get away from those people. I hurried and walked to the car before he left without me. The next bus didn't come for another half hour and I needed to get Christiana's medicine to her by a certain time. He opened the door for me and waited until I got in before getting in the driver seat. Soon as I sat down my body sunk into the seat. It was so soft and comfortable. Whenever I drove somewhere with Angela she made me sit in the trunk of the jeep. She claimed there wasn't enough room for all five of us to sit comfortably.

"So where to?"

"Umm Merrick Pharmacy on Merrick Boulevard."

"Okay, I know where that is." He said pulling into traffic.

We drove quietly for a while, I didn't know what to say so I just stared out the window. I was honestly speechless. What was I supposed to say? I only talked to my stepmom and sisters on the regular. I didn't know how to have a regular conversation with someone. Especially a man as fine as him.

"So are you from New York?" He asked.

"Born in Long Island and now I'm here in Queens." I replied looking at him." What about you?"

"I was raised in Brooklyn. I moved out here to Queens about a three years ago for a job."

"Cool. What do you do?"

"I'm a radiology Tech and I do security on the weekends for a night club. What do you do?" He asked.

"Uh, I'm trying to figure it all out. "I somewhat lied.

"It took me a while to figure out what I wanted to do with my life. I just knew I wanted more than what I had at the time. These days you have so many options so that's always a plus."

"I don't have many options but I know I want more out of life. I just don't know what just yet.' I sighed. "Plus I need the support of my family, they probably wouldn't believe in my dreams anyway."

"You shouldn't worry about other people and what they think. Never do anything that doesn't make you happy. I learned that the hard way."

"What do you mean?" I asked turning my body slightly towards him.

"Why would you do something that doesn't make you happy just to please someone else? You are the one who has to live with the decisions you make and sometimes people give you good advice but it's more so for them than for you. Not everyone has good intentions. Unfortunately, you always learn that part the hard way too."

I was intrigued by him. The way he spoke you could tell he had been through something that caused him pain. I could see it in his eyes. They weren't sparkling like they were when I first saw him. It seemed like he was in deep thought. I wanted to know more about him. Plus it was good to get my head out of the clouds and finally have a decent conversation with someone.

"My whole family wanted me to go to the NFL since I was about seven or eight. They talked about it all my life and I went with it but as I got older I realized the effects football would have on me in the long run. I only agreed to play in college for the scholarship money so I went got my associates. I was going to go for my bachelor's but at that point I was just over it. But my family was so proud of everything I had done up until that point I found it hard to tell them I wasn't going to continue."

"Wow. So what happened?"

"I got my bachelors but it ended there. My family was mad for a while. They tried to get me to get drafted but I refused. Our relationship became strained after that but I was happy. I realized a lot of them looked at me as a chance to get out the hood and that's what drove them to push me so hard. I was in a slump but after a while, I finally started working and doing what I wanted. Best decision of my life."

"Wow. I wish I had your strength and courage." I whispered.

"You can you just have to believe in yourself and put YOU first. What's your story?" He asked.

"Umm, I think you just passed the pharmacy."

"Oh shit. Too busy running my mouth." He laughed.

"It's okay." I giggled.

Low-key I was happy I didn't have to answer his question. I wasn't about to tell this man my whole sob story. He would probably think I'm even crazier than he thought back at the Cleaners. He made a right turn then pulled into the back lot.

"I'll wait for you."

"Oh no, it's fine I live right here." I lied.

"Are you sure? It's no problem."

"Yes of course. You already helped me out tremendously."

"Aight little mama be safe."

"I will and you too," I said. "Thanks again."

Grabbing my stuff I waved goodbye. I made sure to get one last look before disappearing inside. I picked up Christiana's prescription and headed home. When I walked in the door my stepmother was sitting on the couch watching TV. The house was quiet which means the girls weren't here. They would be out for most of the day so I had the house to myself. Angela for the most part left me alone. It was the girls who liked to pick on me.

"Sparkle your home. Perfect."

"Sorry I'm late the bus was crowded." I lied.

"It's fine. Look I'm going out of town for a few days. I already told the girls and you know what you need to do."

"Yes ma'am."

"Good, don't cause any problems and I'll give you your money early. Got it?"

"Yes." I nodded.

"You got my clothes I need it for this weekend?"

"Well uh Jim said the stain in your dress was taking him a while but he should have it by tomorrow."

"Ugh." She rolled her eyes. "Whatever go hang my stuff in the closet and make me some lunch. Then get to the grocery store when you're done."

Walking upstairs I went straight to her room and hung her clothes in the closet like she said. I was glad she was going away maybe I could have a nice quiet week without her. Plus, with her gone the girls would probably go out and I would have the house to myself. Waking into my room I hung my jacket up and took off my shoes. I was going to stay out of everyone's way while Angela was gone. The twenty dollars she gave me each month didn't go far but I always looked forward to it. I would buy my feminine products for the month and some cheap conditioner for my hair. I always tried to save a dollar or two for some candy. Walking back downstairs I walked into the kitchen so I could get started on lunch. Angela had out some ground beef and tomato sauce I guess to make spaghetti. As I prepared my ingredients I thought of the man for earlier. I just realized I didn't get his name, it didn't matter I guess. I knew I would most likely never see him again. It was nice meeting him though.

O'RION

I sat in the parking lot for a few minutes after realizing I never got her name. I waited for a few minutes I had a little time to waste. I didn't want to come off as creepy but I needed to know. It was something about little mama that made me want to know more about her. She was very soft-spoken but I could see the fire in her eyes. She was hurting, it was written all over her. And I couldn't deny how beautiful she was. Shaking the beauty from my head I pulled out of the lot and headed towards my apartment. My girlfriend London's job did a charity event every year and this year I was invited. I didn't want to go but shorty begged me to go and I could never say no to her spoiled ass. I pulled into my complexes lot and grabbed my suit before heading upstairs. When I got to the door I could hear soft music coming from the other side. Pulling out my keys I opened the door and the smell of fried chicken hit my nose. Placing my suit on the couch I went to go find London. I found her in the kitchen wearing nothing but a white silk robe that touched the ground. When she turned towards me I noticed the matching white teddy she had underneath.

"Hey baby." She smiled." I made a quick lunch for us and you're just in time"

"Thanks, babe, I'm starving too," I said leaning in for a kiss.

She kissed me back and then turned to finish lunch. I walked out of the kitchen back into the living room. Grabbing my suit I walked into my bedroom and hung it up so it didn't wrinkle and smell like food. The party wasn't for a few more hours so I had time to relax for a few. I kicked off my sweat suit and put on some basketball shorts. I slid my feet into some Adidas slides and made my way back to the kitchen. Grabbing a beer out the fridge I plopped down on the couch and began channel surfing. I could hear London singing to herself in the kitchen and all I could do was smile. She had a horrible voice but I liked it when she sang to me.

London and I met back in middle school. We were good friends and we dated for a while until she moved away in our sophomore year of high school. We stayed in touch for a few months but then we just fell off. After that, I thought about her from time to time but I never reached out to her again. When I first started working at Zwanger almost three years ago she was the first face I saw and instantly recognized her. We have kind of been together ever since I loved her but I wasn't sure if we were on the same page as far as our future. She wanted to get married but I didn't feel like she was ready to be someone's wife yet. She was very selfish and spoiled and I know I didn't help it cuz I spoiled her but it came to a point where I didn't want to be the only one making sacrifices for our relationship. Don't get me wrong I didn't mind doing what I had to do for my girl I just wanted the same thing in return. It didn't matter how much I talked to her about it she said she would change but she never did. She had been dropping hints about getting engaged and I didn't pay her ass any mind. I knew since a lot of her friends were getting engaged the pressure was on her now but she just wasn't ready. I only wanted to be married once and if we got married now we would end up in somebody's courtroom in five years.

"Babe, you don't hear me?" London yelled waving her hands in my face.

"Sorry I zoned out. What happened?"

"Nothing I was just telling you lunch was ready."

"Thanks, I'm coming," I replied.

Chugging the rest of my beer I got off the couch and we went into the kitchen to eat. London wasn't the best cook but she knew I loved to eat so she learned how to cook simple meals. Today she made fried chicken, yellow rice, and steamed broccoli. We mostly ate out but I appreciated when she did cook it showed me she cared about something other than makeup and shopping. I sat at the table and London brought my plate over and sat it down in front of me. She then sashayed her way to the fridge to get me something to drink. Once she placed my cup of cranberry juice in front of me I dug in.

"So you ready for tonight?" She asked.

"Yea it'll be fun." I shrugged.

"I know you don't want to go but I appreciate it anyway." She smirked.

"You know I can't tell you no anyway." I laughed.

"True." She giggled." I am excited though I mean we haven't been on a date in forever."

"Yes, we have," I said biting into the chicken.

"Name the last time, we did anything. I mean let's be real you are kinda slacking in the romance department lately." She replied side-eyeing me.

"I just took you to Mexico like two months ago and after that we've gone to them wack ass paint and sip classes almost every weekend. We've gone to dinner, I bring you fucking flowers at least once a damn week and you tryna tell me I'm slacking?"

"I want more though O and you know that," She pouted.

"You want what your friends have, I'm almost certain you don't really know what you want."

"And what makes you say that?" She squealed.

She chose today of all days to wanna act up. I should have seen this coming soon as I opened the damn door. I was just excited to get a home-cooked meal that I was blinded. She always wanted to have these conversations and I didn't mind but she could always dish it but could never take it. Every time she complained about something I made sure I fixed it. When I had a problem though she always made it seem like I was buggin and I was tired of the shit honestly.

"Just forget I said anything cuz I can already see where this is going," I said standing up.

I picked up my plate and threw the rest in the garbage. My appetite was ruined. The food wasn't that good anyway so I didn't care. London was right on my heels. I turned around and looked at her before walking away. Every time we argued the same shit happened and honestly it got old a long time ago.

"No, I wanna know what you mean. You said it now be a man and speak on it."

"You really wanna go there?" I dared." First, you didn't want to get married but soon as your sister got engaged you changed your mind and have been nagging me ever since. Just because you keep mentioning it doesn't mean I'm going to do it. Now you wanna have three kids and move to California because your best friend did. I must say you outdid yourself with your latest request and I should have said something then but I was speechless to be honest."

"Oh, yea and what was that?" She said folding her arms across her chest.

"Haven't I always taken good care of you? Don't I always give you what you want within reason?"

"Yes." She nodded.

"Okay then," I said opening the fridge.

"I don't understand."

"Remember two weeks ago when we were laying in bed after we made love and you told me I needed to get a better job so I could support you?"

"Yea and?"

"And then you said my shitty ass job isn't enough to keep you laced in the finest. Last time I checked you had a closet full of designer shoes, that fucking lingerie is from La Perla. Your handbags are expensive you out here rockin bloody shoes and shit and who brought it? I did. Who helped you buy that car? I did. Who paid for all your fucked-up business ideas and didn't get a dime back in return. Who gets to sit at home all day doing nothing? Matter fact who goes to work for ten hours a week and then sits on her ass? You do. But yet you do nothing for yourself or me but you expect me to? You know why your friends are moving up in the world and you're not?"

"Yes, O'Rion I would love to know." She challenged.

"Because you're not about shit."

"Fuck you O. I do a lot for your ass and in return, I want to be your wife."

"A marriage is a partnership. Why would I marry you when I'm bringing everything to the table? The chairs, the table cloth and the got damn forks and knives. You got a lot of growing up to do and I swear I be trying but you're so caught up in yourself you don't realize it. I'm not trying to be mean but I'm tired of holding it in." I shrugged.

"So why be with me O?"

"Obviously I love you and we've been together for a minute now and in my heart, I believe you can be better. I've been working with you this long haven't I?"

"I'm not some kind of project that you work on when you feel like it. I have feelings and emotions also."

"And so do I but you never seemed to care about that. I'm always walking on eggshells around you because you're so selfish you don't see that what you do hurts the people around you."

"I've never done anything to hurt you and you know it."

"Just because it's not physical doesn't mean it doesn't hurt."

"Well then tell me what I've done to you."

"It hurts me to know I gave up and changed my life around for someone who can't even give me half the curtesy I give to you. We started cool everything was great. I had my best friend back and I was starting a new job life was great. Three months later you had nowhere to go so of course I moved you in here and I thought we would grind together to reach the top. You quit your job without telling me and just expected me to take care of you, you fucking lied about it and if I didn't wake up I would have still thought you just got fired. Do you see how little shit like that is fucked up?"

"I apologized," London whined.

"Yea and then continued to do little shit behind my back like I wouldn't find out."

"I'm not doing it to hurt you but you know my past."

"You know mine also but that's not an excuse. What would you do if we broke up? Where would you go? How would you survive?"

"I have a family."

"See that's the problem. Stop relying on people to get shit done and go out there and do it yourself. You don't have to punch somebody else's clock, you can go out and create your own business or whatever but do something for yourself."

"Whatever O'Rion," She waved me off.

"We don't gotta talk about it anymore cuz I'm tired of talking and nothing changing but I'm telling you now Lon get ya shit together." I snapped before walking off.

I walked into my bedroom and closed the door behind me. Plopping down on my bed I ran my fingers through my hair. I swear I grew a grey hair every time I talked to this girl. I was starting to think deeper into why I was really with her. I laid down and stared up at the ceiling trying to relax my mind. I might've said some fucked up things but she needed to hear it. I was serious when I said I would bounce. I loved London like I said but I didn't know if I was in love with her. I blamed myself though for putting up with the shit this long. After tonight I would rethink this relationship, let's just hope we can get through tonight first.

After agreeing to put all the bull shit behind us for the night London and I finally arrived at the party. The whole ride here was awkward as fuck but she better lose the attitude before we got in here. I pulled my car into the lot so the valet could take it. Running around to the passenger side I opened the door for London. Placing her hand into my awaiting palm she got out. She looked so beautiful tonight and I hoped we could enjoy it and then each other after. She wore a red dress that stopped just above her knees. The black heels she wore made her legs look nice and long. A black fur coat hung loosely off her shoulders as if it wasn't cold out. As usual, her hair and makeup were flawless. Her ebony hair fell in loose curls around her heart-shaped face. The moonlight reflected off her mocha-colored skin highlighting her high cheekbones. Walking arm and arm into the party hall I felt like I was on the red carpet. London stopped and spoke to almost everyone on our way inside. Once we reached where the party was being held London let go of my arm and ran off to go speak to someone. I shook my head and decided to head to the bar.

On my way to the bar, I took in the décor. There was a big stage that swallowed up the room with little table surrounding it. Silver and Blue was the color scheme for tonight. There were balloons at every table and some floating on the ceiling. Everyone was dressed in there Sundays best tonight. Making my way over to the bar I sat down, looking around I noticed something. Several other men were sitting alone at the bar. I'm guessing their wives left them alone too. The bartender came to take my drink order. I ordered a double shot of Hennessey and took it back as soon as he placed in front of me. Turning around to face the dance floor I tried looking for London but I didn't see her. I sat there and bopped my head to the music, if she didn't want to spend some time with me then I would at least entertain myself. I never finished my food from earlier and I was starving. I saw a waiter go by with a plate of shrimp cocktail. I waved him down and grabbed me a few pieces. Dinner wasn't until eight-thirty and it was only going on seven-thirty. I ordered another shot this time a single one since I was driving tonight.

"Girlfriend left you alone also?" I heard.

"Yup," I replied.

The man sat down next to me and ordered himself a drink. He was a short white man maybe in his earlier forties or late thirties.

"I don't even know why I came," He spoke. "It's the same shit every year."

"Damn really? This is my first time."

"This is my fourth. MY wife comes and soon as we enter she

runs away to do god knows what. I usually sit at the bar and then find her right before dinner."

"Damn. What is she doing?"

"Her and the girls usually go to the bathroom and take selfies and shit."He shrugged.

"Figures." I laughed. "I'm O'Rion by the way."

"Larry." He said reaching out to shake my hand.

Larry and I sat around eating and talking until it was time for dinner. Larry left to go find his wife and I went to go find London. I searched everywhere for her but I couldn't find her. I tried calling her phone but she didn't answer. I figured she would meet me back at the table so I started making my way to find our table. On my way back I heard a woman crying uncontrollably. Then I heard a familiar voice. It was London. I followed the cries to a hallway by the ladies' room.

"Please stop crying," London said.

"I just don't understand why you would come here with him. You told me you were leaving him." The woman replied.

My heart sunk, how could London do this to me? I gave her whatever her heart desired physically and emotionally. If she didn't want to be with me she could have just told me. Never in a million years would I have expected this.

"I am baby I am. It's just hard. I don't have anywhere to go and we can't move in together yet."

"I don't care London, it's been almost a year, and six months ago you said give you six months and then you show up with him?"

"I'm doing all I can Keisha," London replied.

"But not enough."

"What do you want me to do Key? Huh? I've been taking the money he gives me and saving it plus my little checks but we live in fucking New York it's expensive as fuck out here."

"I don't know what you want me to tell you, Lon. If you're not going to do it then we should just end this."

"No no baby I'm going to do it just give me time."

"I'm done giving you time. Your family doesn't know you're gay and I'm fine with that but I'm not fine with you still being with him. I understand he has been there for you and supported you but what about me?"

"It's not that easy to just walk away from someone I've been friends with since we were younger, he's more than my boyfriend he's my best friend."

"Do you still love him?"

"I do but I'm not in love with him. Baby, I love you and I'm trying my hardest just be patient with me."

"I don't know if I can. I'm tired London, I'm so tired."

"One more week and I'll do it. I just need time to come up with a new plan."

"Fine one week." She replied.

"How about we end it tonight?" I announced stepping into the hallway.

"W-what are you doing here?" London stuttered.

"Well dinner was starting so I came to look for you and this is what I find? You could have just told me instead of cheating on me." I yelled.

"Don't talk to her like that." The women spat.

"Key," London said holding up her hand to silence her.

She rolled her eyes and crossed her hands over her chest. While London sat there with tears in her eyes my mind was racing. Why didn't I see the signs before? Was this all because I wouldn't marry her? I had so many questions but on the other hand, I wanted to get out of here.

"Look London if this is what you want then fine but don't come to me when shit goes wrong."

"Maybe if you would have married her ass and treated her better then this wouldn't be happening." The girl spat.

"Key!" London screamed.

"What?" She shrugged. "It's true."

"O I'm so sorry. I didn't want you to find out like this. You've been there for me for all these years I didn't want to hurt you."

"Save the bull shit for someone else London."

I turned to walk away and she grabbed my arm. I looked down at her hand and yanked my arm away. I was disgusted. Not because she was in a lesbian relationship but because she lied to me and she stole from me. This wasn't the girl I knew and I was disappointed.

"Have your shit out my house by the morning," I said and walked away.

"O'Rion come back please." She cried.

"Go after him then since you want him so bad." Her girlfriend screamed.

"Key just shut up." London cried.

I got out of there as fast as I could before I went back up there to give them both a piece of my mind. Sprinting to the valet I hoped he hurried before London decided to come down. When he pulled up I met him on the driver side and handed him a twenty-dollar tip before getting in my car and speeding off. I drove straight home and changed out of my clothes. I packed a quick bag and got back in my car. I had no idea where I was going to go but I didn't want to be alone before I did something I would regret. I was more mad than anything. I was mad that she stole from me and lied to me. Mad that I didn't see the signs. My phone rung snapping me out of my thoughts. I looked at the screen on my dashboard and saw it was my cousin Tyree calling.

"Wassup boy?" I said.

"Aint shit my G. what you fucking with?"

"Nun right now just driving around."

"Oh, I thought you had that thing tonight with London."

"I did." I sighed.

"Ahh man, what happened?"

"Where you at? I'll come to you."

"I'm at the crib with Jolie come by we ain't doing shit."

"Aight bet I'll be there in ten I'm not far from your house."

"Say less." He said and hung up.

I pulled up to his house shortly after. Little did he know I was staying here with him tonight. Tyree was my cousin on my mom's side. We grew up together and had always been close. Even when he chose the streets and I chose college that was still my ace. I got out of the car and grabbed my bag of clothes and my phone. Before I could knock on the door his wife Jolie opened the door. She smiled and ushered me inside. They had the music bumpin and I could smell food. When the smell hit my nose my stomach growled

"Hey Jo," I said hugging her.

"Hey, Ry. How you doing?"

"Man if you only knew."

"Ahh shit London trouble?"

"You know it. Where's Ty?"

"He's coming he ran to make a punch real quick. Get comfortable are you hungry?"

"I'm starving."

"Okay, I'll make you a plate." She laughed.

"Thanks, Jo."

I put my bag down by the couch and sat down. Leaning my head back on the couch inhaled and let it out. I was trying to keep calm. I just needed time to figure this all out. Jolie came back with a huge plate of food. She had mac and cheese, fried chicken cabbage, and cornbread.

"Damn Jo." I smiled.

"You know your cousin greedy." She laughed.

"Don't be talking bout me girl," Tyree yelled walking into the house.

"Wassup my G," I said standing up to give him dap.

"I see you got your bags." He said pointing to them." What happened?"

"London's been cheating on me," I admitted sitting back down.

"Oh no." Jolie gasped.

"Yea and get this shit. With a woman."

"Get the fuck outta here," Tyree shouted.

"Deadass."

"Wow, that's wild as fuck."

"And she was stealing from me so she could move out to be with her."

"You want me to fuck her up? I retired from the street life but you're my favorite cuz." Jolie said.

"Nah Jo, London would just call the cops."

"You know I don't give a fuck."

"I know," I laughed.

"So now what?" Tyree asked.

"I don't know, I told her to have her shit out my house by the morning. I'm not even hurt I'm mad that she lied and stole from me."

"Well you know you can stay here for a few days if you need," Jolie said.

"Thanks."

"Look eat your food and relax. I'll go change the sheets in the guest room and you can go relax."

"Thanks, Jo I appreciate it."

"No problem." She replied as she walked away.

"You sure you good cuz? I know you loved her."

"That's the thing I mean I loved her but I haven't been in love with her for a while."

"That explains why you're not hurt."

"I guess so. I didn't even wait for an explanation cuz, I just dipped. She's not the same girl I got with three years ago and before I did something I had to go."

"I feel you. Wanna drink?"

"Yea let me get a double shot of Henny."

"Aight bet."

Tyree came back a second later with the whole bottle. I shook my head and took my glass and poured me a shot. Tyree and I sat up for hours drinking and talking. He took my mind off of the whole situation. I was surprised he didn't shit on London. Most of my family didn't like her and now that my head was a little clearer I could see why.

"Aight my nigga I'm out. Jo and I got somethings to do in the morning. You should come with us to this party her friend throwing It'll take your mind off the bull shit."

"When?"

"This weekend."

"I don't know cuz I'll think about it. I got somethings to figure out I might just lay low for a while."

"Aight but if you change your mind let me know.

"Aight bet."

"Aight cuz good looks I appreciate it."

"No doubt bro this is what family is for."

I gave Ty dap and he disappeared into the room. I sat there for a moment and finished my drink. Alone with my thoughts, I replayed everything over in my mind from the last year. I couldn't pinpoint where we went wrong. Before I drove myself crazy I decided to go to bed.

Sparkle

"Wake up ugly," Christiana yelled.

Jumping up I screamed before realizing what was going on. I thought they were trying to attack me in my sleep. Grabbing my glasses off my night table I put them on and stared at Christiana. She had a big smile on her face and I just knew something was up.

"What Chris?" I groaned.

"We're having a party."

"I don't have any damn friends so what that gotta do with me?"

"Who else is gonna cook and shit duh?"

"What are you having a party for?"

"Just to have one. With mom gone for the week why not?"

"Is that what yal have been planning all week?"

"Yup. Now enough questions I need you to go to the store and get the decorations, cups, and shit. Me and the twins are going food shopping. So get up and go. Here's fifty dollars and don't forget anything." Christiana rambled.

Petting me on my head she hopped up and left the room. I rolled my eyes and laid back down. Looking at my clock it was eight forty-five. I still didn't understand why she wanted to have a party. I figured my stepmother was gone since they were talking about a party so openly. She rarely went away for days but when she did they always did something dumb and somehow, I was always the one to fix it. I don't know why though. They treated me like shit the moment my father left and if I could go I would. I would go far away and not come back. I would be something in life and do the things I've dreamed of. I resented my father so much for taking me away from my mom and leaving me with these people. If I did get away I would never talk to him again. Getting out of bed I grabbed my shower caddy and went to go shower. Today was going to be long so I hurried up so I could head to the store and be back by the time they came back.

I WAS RUNNING AROUND THE KITCHEN PREPPING THE FOOD for later. The girls were out finding outfits for the night. Ever since they told me about this party they've been driving me crazy. This morning I went to the ninety-nine-cent store and when I got home Christiana attacked me for taking too long. Meanwhile, she got home after me. Then she told me tonight I would have to tend to their guests. I had planned to stay in my room and reading a book I borrowed from the library. But no, these hoes couldn't cook or do nothing without Sparkle. It was going on five-thirty and the party started around eight. The mac and cheese, potato salad, and deviled eggs were done. I had the ribs slow-cooking since this morning. The BBQ chicken and meatballs were ready to come out of the oven. All I had to do now was make cupcakes. Christiana and the twins had some of her friends bringing food which I was grateful for. I pulled out all my ingredients for my red velvet cake. I had to make fifty red velvet cupcakes and fifty chocolate cupcakes plus I had to frost them all in less than two hours. I quickly made my batter and filled the cupcake liners with red velvet and chocolate batter. Christiana's boyfriend Joel was in and out of the living room to his car setting up the bar. He was always nice to me and got on Chris about being mean to me. When he was around she was the sweetest thing so I never minded when he came.

"Wassup Sparkle?" Joel asked when he walked into the kitchen.

"Hey Joel. How are you?" I replied placing the chicken on the table.

"I'm coolin'. You need help?"

"Nah I can handle it. Thanks though." I smiled.

I heard Christiana's loud voice soon as she entered the house. She walked into the kitchen and pushed a bag into my chest.

"You won't be embarrassing me tonight so we brought you this dress." She said.

"Oh, wow thank you."

Pulling it out the bag the first thing I noticed was how soft it felt against my fingertips. It was a long sleeve black velvet pleated dress. Putting it up to my chest I noticed it came down to about my knees. It was kind of short and that made me nervous. Angela didn't want me showing any skin at all which wasn't fair since the girls got to wear these short ass shorts that showed their ass cheeks.

"I love it thank you but-"

"Girl she ain't here so chill out. Maybe you can finally get you a man." She laughed.

"Probably not." Ava laughed coming into the kitchen.

"True." Christiana agreed.

I rolled my eyes and put the dress back in the bag. I placed the bag on the kitchen chair and checked on my cupcakes. Once they were done I took those out and placed them on the counter to cool. Christiana was following me around the kitchen watching my every move.

"I didn't burn them so can you back up please?"

"I'm just checking don't get smart." She replied plucking me on my forehead.

She laughed on her way out to the living room. I was glad Joel was here tonight it should go good. Hopefully. Filling up the next back of cupcake liners I put those in the oven and started frosting the other cupcakes. I frosted the red velvet cupcakes with cream cheese frosting and sprinkled red sprinkles on it. For the chocolate cupcake I did a chocolate frosting. They looked amazing and I wanted to try one. Since I couldn't right now I took one of each and wrapped them up. Placing them in the bag with my dress I ran them upstairs to my bedroom. I pulled the dress out the bag again and held it against my body. Looking in the mirror I admired myself. I couldn't wait to put this on, I thought I would look great in it. I still had about an hour left before the party so I started to get ready. I hung the dress up and then looked out my window. Christiana and the twins were outside helping Joel so I ran to her room and stole one of her razors. I ran back to my room and hid it under my pillow just in case. Running back downstairs I pulled out my last batch of cupcakes and set them to cool.

"Sparkle come set up the sternos they need to be lit soon so the food will be hot," Christiana yelled.

I rolled my eyes and began stacking the aluminum pans so I can carry more and make less trips. I brought everything out and Joel helped me set everything up so I could have time to get dolled up. Christiana and the twins were sitting on the couch smoking. I hated the smell of it but I did it once when they forced me and I kinda liked it.

"Sparkle get off my man dick and go do something. Don't you have cupcakes to do or something?"

"Chris shut up." Joel snapped.

"Why should I? Every time you come over she be all over you. I mean let's be real sparkle you could never pull a man like Joel even on your best day."

"You outta line." Joel gritted.

"Its fine Joel, I'm used to it." I sighed.

I tried not to let them see me upset so I just walked away. I ran up to my room and screamed into my pillow. I hated living here and I wish my life was different. I wish my mother wasn't in jail. My life would be so much better if she was here. Ever since my mom got arrested I had only spoken to her a few times and that was in the beginning. My father moved us and made sure I lost all contact with her. Two years later he was married and we were living with Angela and her kids. I had no idea where my mom could even be. When we left she hadn't been sentenced yet so there was no telling where she was or if she was even alive right now. With no access to the internet finding her was impossible. I pushed that to the back of my mind and started getting ready. I took my razor and my hair products with me to the bathroom. Usually, I wrote my hair in a puff but today I was going to try something different.

———

THE PARTY WAS IN FULL EFFECT. I COULD HEAR MUSIC blasting and people laughing. I sat in my room pacing, I was full of nerves. I thought I looked great but what if people laughed. The dress fit me nice and snug and showed off my body which was usually hidden under baggy sweat pants and a T-shirt. I tried a wash and go something I saw in a natural hair magazine when Christiana would take me with her to the hair salon. My natural curls hung just above my shoulders, with a part down the middle. On my feet, I wore some black flats that I had from when we went to church for Easter last year. I felt amazing but I just couldn't get over my nerves. I knew they would be calling me soon so I can tend to their guest. I inhaled deeply and walked out of my room and downstairs. There were about ten people in the living some sitting down smoking. I recognized some of them from previous parties. The girls waved and the guys nodded. I waved back and kept it moving to the kitchen. They had the kitchen blocked off so nobody would go in there. I moved the barricades and found Christiana and Joel in the kitchen.

"Sparkle, you actually look nice." She smiled.

I could tell from her eyes she was drunk already. Instead of being upset I decided to take that as a compliment. The pause she took told me she was tryna be funny but whatever. Little did she know she looked like a pear with a face.

"Thank you," I replied.

"Yea Spark, I agree," Joel said.

Thanks."

"Look start bringing out food and set it on the table. Make sure everyone has a cup and if it's empty refill it. Bring the garbage around and take people's plates if it's empty. Don't forget about the people in the basement either. Got it?"

"Yup." I nodded.

I scurried away and started doing what she said. I started bringing pans out and set them over the sternos. I had set the table up nicely. The girls wanted everything gold and black so those were the colors of the forks and cups as well. I was running around filling cups and taking coats. More and more people came as time went on. The lights were dim now to set the mood a little. A lot of people came with their boyfriends. They were cuddled up in every corner kissing and grinding on each other. I tried to stay out of there way as much as possible. Everyone seemed to love the food, as soon as I put out more people flocked to it eating it all up. It made me happy that people were enjoying it. Angela always talked shit about my food even though she would eat it all up too. I took the opportunity to get some air so I grabbed my coat and the garbage and headed outside for a few. Once I stepped outside I let the cool air fill my lungs. It was hot as hell in that house. Dumping the garbage in the bin I stood there for a few before going back inside.

O'RION

I SAT IN THE CORNER OF THE PARTY SIPPING ON MY DRINK. This wasn't really my scene but it was better than sitting in the house angry all day. Jolie had convinced me to come out for a few just to get some free drinks and shit so I said fuck it. I didn't have anything else to do tonight. I hadn't seen them since I got here but I didn't mind. I wanted to be left to my thoughts anyway. I still hadn't talked to London but for some reason she was on my mind. She had been blowing up my phone for the past week but finally stopped yesterday. She still hadn't gotten her shit out of my house yet so I've been staying with Jolie and Ty until she did. I stayed up most of the night thinking about where everything went wrong and I realized I wasn't the problem but I did help enable her. That was where I fucked up at. It is what it is though one day maybe we could talk but for now I was ready to move on. I loved her but I wasn't in love with her and I would never want to hold anybody hostage. Except for myself, I think I've known for a while I was just comfortable with her after being together for so long. Looking around the room I noticed there were a lot of couples. I noticed a few single people but nobody caught my eye. I had only been here an hour and I was ready to go. I searched the room for my cousin but I couldn't find him. I would text him when I got in my car to let him know I left. I started making my way towards the door when I heard someone scream. It wasn't even a scream as if they were in danger. It was more like an obnoxious screech. As I looked back the music cut off and that's when shit got real. The room split down the middle as everyone moved over so they could get a good look.

"You dumb bitch. You dropped my fucking cupcakes." The girl screamed again.

I couldn't hear what the other girl was saying but she looked like she was apologizing. She bent down and started picking up cupcakes off the floor. I figured the girl that was screaming was just drunk and overreacting. Everyone at the party was laughing and snickering as the girl scrambled to pick up the cupcakes. I shook my head and kept walking towards the door. I felt bad for the girl it wasn't that deep.

"Hurry the fuck up." She yelled. "I should make your dumbass go in there and make some more. I swear you are the stupidest fucking person I ever met. I wish your fucking crackhead mother wasn't in jail maybe she would have come to take your stupid ass a long time ago."

When she said that everyone in the room gasped. The girl in the black dress stood up and balled up her fist. I felt bad she had to be embarrassed like that especially over some fucking cupcakes. Nobody deserved that kind of treatment.

"Don't talk about my mother," She yelled.

"Fuck you and your funky ass mother. Clean up these damn cupcakes and go make some more."

"No!" The girl yelled back. "I'm tired of your shit."

"Don't you dare tell me no again." She yelled and backhanded her.

The girl's glasses flew off her face and landed by my feet. I picked them up and started walking towards her to return them. Before I could the girl ran off towards the back of the house. I ran after her to make sure she was okay. Nobody else seemed to care so it was the least I could do.

"Turn the music back on." I heard as I approached the door.

The party seemed to pick up right where it left off. I walked out of the half-open door, the brisk air hitting me hard. It was dark out so I couldn't really see but I could hear her sobs. I was still shocked at what I just witnessed. All that over some damn cupcakes? I hoped it was more to the story cuz if not these niggas was crazy. I just wanted to make sure she was okay since nobody else did. Following her cries, I found her on the side of the house crying into her hands.

"Hey are you okay?" I asked softly trying not to scare her.

"I-I'm fine." She replied wiping her eyes.

"You sure? Here I got your glasses."

"Thank you." She said turning around to face me.

When I saw her my mouth dropped. This was the girl from the other day. I never thought I would see her again and here she was. Ever since the day I met her I had been thinking about her. I tried to push her out of my head since I had a girlfriend but she was beautiful I couldn't help myself. Not just her physical features but her spirit. I didn't talk to her long but her aura was electrifying.

"What?" She asked.

"You don't remember me? "

"Its dark out here and I don't have my glasses on. I can't really see anything."

"Oh, shit I'm sorry here." I said passing her the glasses.

She wiped her eyes again and put them on. I noticed she was shivering so I took off my jacket and began to wrap it around her shoulders.

"No, I couldn't take your coat. I shouldn't have come outside like this. I'm so stupid." She babbled.

"Relax its fine. I have another coat in my car come on."

I grabbed her hand and took her to my car. Unlocking the door I opened the passenger side door for her and then ran around to the other side. Getting my coat out of the back seat I put it on then got in the car with her.

"Remember me now?" I smiled.

"Yes." She blushed. "What are you doing here?"

"My cousin invited me. What are you doing here?"

"I live here." She said bowing her head.

"Who was that girl?"

"Oh, Christiana? She's my step sister."

"Wow. I never thought I'd see you again. I realized after you left I never got your name."

"It's Sparkle." She sniffled.

"That's a beautiful name." I replied." I'm O'Rion."

"Like the constellation?"

"Exactly." I laughed.

"I like it."

"Thanks."

She didn't look how she did when I first met her. Her hair was different, it fell perfectly around her face in a mass of curls. The dress she wore showed off her womanly figure. Even though her legs were trembling I couldn't help but notice them either way. I had a thing for nice legs. She shyly stared out the window, sulking in her own self-pity. When I first met her I just thought she was shy but now I see she was being abused and it explained it all.

"Why do you put up with that?" I asked.

Turning to face me she opened her mouth to speak but then closed it. Biting on her bottom lip she nervously began to shake her legs. Reaching my hand out I placed it on her arm. When we touched I felt a spark throughout my body. That was something I had never experienced before. I felt her body relax just from my touch.

"Just relax," I whispered.

"Why are you being so nice to me?" She asked.

"I'm just a nice person." I chuckled. "Now answer my question."

"I-I have nowhere else to go. They're all I got."

"Where are your parents? If you don't want to answer that's fine."

"My mom is in prison and my father is overseas. I live here with my stepmother and her three children."

"And your father doesn't care if you're being abused?"

"I'm not being abused." She nervously laughed.

"Sparkle I can tell you are. Look at what happened."

She let out a sigh and then she started crying. I hated seeing women cry. Growing up I saw my mom crying plenty of nights over my father and just life in general. I was young and there was nothing I could do about it but I promised my mom when I was younger that I would look out for her when I got older. I made sure to keep that promise too.

"I'm sorry." She said." I don't even know you and here I am crying."

"Stop apologizing Sparkle it's fine."

"When my mother got arrested my father took me and ran. I used to live in long island my father wanted to stay in New York just far enough that my mom couldn't find us. Three months after we moved to Brooklyn he met Angela my stepmother and six months later we moved to Queens to live with her and her kids. Two years had passed they were married and this was my new family. I mean at first things were good. We all got along and I was happy even though I missed my mom. Eventually, my father went back to the work and I was left here. That's when the abuse started happening from everyone. "

"What did your father say when you told him?" I asked.

"When I first told him, he said I was probably being bad." She shrugged." I told him a few more times but he never believed me so I stopped telling him."

"Damn that's fucked up."

"Yea it is. He wasn't always like that though when him and my mom were together they were happy. At least to me. It wasn't until she went to jail that he changed. Once he left I became their maid. I cooked and cleaned, I did there Laundry and the grocery shopping. I went to school and came straight home to get started on dinner. I was the first one up before school to make breakfast and the last one to sleep. Once I graduated I was only allowed to leave home if I was running errands for the house and usually Angela is right outside waiting for me. They're all I have and with no money I'm stuck."

"Have you thought about just leaving?"

"All the time of course but how would I survive? I have no money or any job experience. Who's going to hire me?"

"I know I don't know you but you've got to get out of here. Stop letting people hold you back."

"It's easier said than done." She replied.

"I know and I can help you, maybe get you a job at my job as a receptionist or something."

"Why?"

"What do you mean why?"

"Why would you want to help me? You don't know me from a hole in the wall. I'm just some weird girl you met in the cleaners."

"You're far from weird Sparkle and because I hate to see people down. Plus do you remember what I told you the day I met you?'

"Yes." She nodded.

"I wish I would have had help myself or at least someone to give me advice."

"I don't know what to say. I'm not used to people being nice to me besides Mr. Jim and Chris's boyfriend. All I have is myself and if you can't tell I'm awkward. I wouldn't even know what to do or say."

"You're talking to me just fine."

"True. I guess I feel comfortable around you and I don't know why."

"You gotta be more confident and believe in yourself. I know I don't know you but I believe in you."

"You do?" she squealed.

Tears began to fall again and I realized just how broken this girl was. Being taken away from her mom and having an abusive family and a dad who didn't care was fucked up. I didn't have a dad growing up but I was loved by everyone in my family. I had support from those around me but she didn't. She had no one and that shit was sad. It was making me regret falling out with my family for all those months.

"Of course I do. We'll figure something out. I can give you my number or I can take yours and we can keep in contact."

"I uh-uh don't have a phone."

"Seriously?"

"Yea I don't have much of anything.

"Okay, we'll figure something out don't worry."

"I don't know what to say. I'm sorry I don't mean to just put this all on you."

"Stop apologizing you have nothing to be sorry for."

We sat in the car for hours talking about everything. She told me more about her life and I told her a little about mine. I was pretty boring so it wasn't much to tell honestly. I listened to her every word because her story was sad but interesting at the same time. I found out that she was twenty years old and she loved to write short stories to help her deal with her home life. She was so much stronger than she realized. Even with everything she was going through she was feisty and funny. She let her wall down and was just herself. Around one a.m the police came and shut down the party. Sparkle and I laughed from my car as all the people made their way to their cars. Even when the party was over we kept talking. We watched her stepsisters bring out the trash and we cracked jokes the whole time. She was funny as hell and had such a big personality but it was hidden by fear. I was glad she felt comfortable around me to let go and be free. I could only imagine what she felt like on a regular basis living here. I had a long day and decided to go home. It was going on two am and I had work. I was glad I came to the party, I could only imagine what would have happened to Sparkle if I didn't. I walked her to her front door and pulled her into my arms. I just felt compelled to hug her. I knew she needed it badly. She smelled amazing like a euphoria of fruits from coconuts to mango. That spark shot through my body again. I wonder if she felt it too. Smiling at me she gave me my jacket back and disappeared into the house. Walking down the stairs I looked back at the house before getting in my car.

"Wow."

Taking the long way home I finally pulled up to my complex. I parked my car and got out. The whole ride home I couldn't stop thinking about Sparkle. She was amazing and she didn't even know it. The fear brought on by her family washed away today. It was only temporary but she deserved permanent peace.

Fear made you a different person I wondered what the 100% fearless Sparkle would be like. Unlocking my apartment door I was surprised to hear voices. I closed the door behind me and followed the noises to my bedroom. When I swung open the door London and her girlfriend screamed.

"O'Rion you scared us." She snapped.

"What are you doing here?" I asked ignoring her statement.

"I-I uhh came to get my stuff."

"Okay, but why at two am and why bring her?" I said pointing to her girl.

"Don't be mad cuz you lost your girl to a bitch." She smiled.

"You can have her I don't care about that, it's a respect thing. But then again she did me dirty so obviously she doesn't respect me." I said matter factly.

"Don't do that Ry." London pleaded.

"Look just hurry up and get your shit and get out. I'll be in the living room and don't take anything that doesn't belong to you." I said walking out.

I could hear her girlfriend mumbling something but I didn't care. I just wanted them gone and London out of my life for good. I thought seeing her would bring up some feelings but it just made me angrier and I didn't understand why. I finally admitted to myself that I wasn't in love with her anymore so why was I so angry? After a half-hour, London finally came out of the room with her little friend close behind. She had two duffle bags full of stuff and a suitcase. She must've been here for a while if that's all she had. They started walking to the door and then stopped. London whispered something in her ear and she looked at her like she was crazy before opening the door and leaving. London turned to face me and stared at me.

"I'm really am sorry Ry. I didn't want it to go down like this. I hope we can still be friends." She said.

"No thank you." I replied dryly."

"Come on O'Rion don't be childish." She had the nerve to say.

"I'm not I don't see the point in being friends. If you really were my friend you would have told me instead of playing me."

"You're being dramatic."

"Of course I am," I replied.

"Seriously Ry. We both know we weren't happy so why act like this?"

"If you were so unhappy why cheat and not just leave me. This is why I don't wanna fuck with you at all. You only stayed so you can steal money from me to pay for your lesbian affair."

"Don't do that." She gritted.

"Do what? Tell the truth. I did everything for you. When your own family stopped fucking with you I was there. When you were homeless I moved you in with me. I brought you all the shit you have now. You were nothing before me but I hope you become something without me. I'm not cold-hearted I wish you the best in life but when shit goes wrong don't come to me."

"I won't." She huffed.

"Whatever. Anything else?"

"Fuck you Ry." She said storming out of my apartment.

Shaking my head I got up to close and lock the door. London had some nerve but karma was a bitch so I wasn't worried. Walking to my room I went straight to the bathroom and turned on the shower. Throwing my clothes in the hamper I stepped into the shower. As I washed up thoughts of Sparkle consumed me. She was so fragile and I couldn't help to feel bad for her but at the same time, I wanted to know her more. After what I witnessed I needed to help her I just didn't know how. In the morning, I was going to call my grandma to see what resources she could find her. Washing the soap off my body I stepped out of the shower. I through on some boxers and got in bed. Today was long and tiring, I tried closing my eyes but every time I did I saw Sparkles face. I saw her curly hair and big bright eyes very clear. It was like she was in front of me smiling so vividly.

THINGS AROUND THE HOUSE HAD BEEN SO AWKWARD THE PAST few days. Neither Christiana nor the twins bothered me and I stayed in my room away from them. Once I heard them leave the house I finally emerged from my room to make myself some lunch. I decided on a quick turkey sandwich and some chips. After quickly making my sandwich I went back to my room to hideout. I didn't want to see any of them today. Christiana embarrassed me so bad and if it was up to me I would never show my face again. I tossed and turned all night trying to figure out why. It had to be more than just about the cupcakes. Then again when she got drunk she did tend to get more violent. Either way, it was unacceptable for her to be putting her hands on me. Especially in front of other people. From the mom to her offspring none of them had any class or couth. I tried to get that image out of my head but all I kept hearing was the giggles of people around me. I never expected people to help me but I also didn't expect people to stand there laughing like that shit was funny. The only thing that kept my spirits up was O'Rion. Although I hated he saw that unfold I was just glad he was there to comfort me. He didn't even know me but he was there for me and I would forever be grateful. I kept hearing his words of encouragement over and over in my mind. It sparked something inside of me and it made me want to keep fighting. If a stranger could believe in me why can't I believe in myself?

"Sparkle!" my stepmother yelled from downstairs.

Sighing I got out of bed and went downstairs. When the fuck did she get home? Besides the incident at the party this weekend everything had been good without her here. She was sitting on the couch with a short brown fur on. Even her hair was different. She usually kept it straight but today it was in a nice pixie cut. I couldn't believe she cut her hair. Her hair actually looked good on her. I loved my natural curls and would never get a perm but the style was nice. Standing in front of her I waited for her to speak. She looked me up and down before passing me the phone. Confused I took it anyway.

"Hello?"

"Hey baby girl, it's your dad."

"Oh hi daddy," I mumbled.

"Just wanted to check in with you. I've been really busy these past few days. Sorry I didn't call before."

"It's okay. Is everything okay over there?" I asked.

"Yea it's great. I can't talk long I just wanted you to know I love you and I'll see you soon."

"Yea love you too."

"I sent Angel two hundred dollars for you. Make sure you buy yourself something nice. Christmas will be here before you know it."

"I will dad thanks. Bye."

Handing the phone back to Angela I started walking away when she grabbed my arm. It was bad enough I had to fake like I wanted to talk to his ass now she wanted to talk. It was bad enough he only called me once a week but him and Angel talked almost every day. I sat there nervously looking around the house. I didn't know what she wanted I just hoped I wasn't in trouble. Hearing a horn I looked out the window to see Christiana getting dropped off by Joel. Rolling my eyes I waited for Angela to get off the phone so I could get out of everyone's way. Christiana came into the house and plopped down on the couch next to her mom. She had this look on her face but I couldn't decipher what it meant. After a few more minutes of standing there, she finally got off the phone.

"Hey baby girl." She smiled at Christiana." You had a good week while I was gone?"

"Yes it was great but I missed you so much." She pouted.

I wanted to throw up in my mouth. They were both so obnoxious. Chris was twenty-three years old acting like a damn child. While Angela just soaked it all up. It was all just sickening, to be honest.

"I missed you too baby. Anything happen while I was gone?"

Christiana looked at me and smirked. There goes my money for the month. The little twenty dollars I got once a month was literally everything to me. It wasn't much but it was mine.

"Well, everything was good until we had a party and Sparkle fucked it up." She sighed.

"All I did was drop the cupcakes I MADE!"

"Shut up Sparkle." My stepmother snapped." Go on Chris."

"Well, yea she dropped them and then made a big scene. She yelled at me too."

Angela looked over at me and shook her head. These two couldn't be for real. Sometimes I felt I was living in an alternate universe. They would complain and Angela would act so appalled. They all had some deep-rooted issues.

"In my defense you talked about my mom." I shrugged.

"I don't give a fuck what she said. You don't talk back. I'm getting real tired of the disrespect, get your shit together. You understand? "

When I didn't respond she hopped up and got all in my face. Her nostrils flared as her chest rose up and down seething with anger. I seriously thought there was something wrong with all of them.

"I said do you understand Sparkle? Answer me when I talk to you."

"Yes I understand," I mumbled.

"Better had! now go do something productive and get the fuck out of my face. And since you don't listen you won't be getting your monthly money and you damn sure ain't getting the two hundred your father sent for you either. You can kiss all that shit goodbye."

Christiana snickered in the background. I shot her a look that could kill. It was all her fault. I already knew she wouldn't give me two hundred dollars but now she was taking the twenty I got every month from me. That's all the money I had besides my secret coin stash. How would I buy my feminine products now I thought walking into the kitchen. This shit wasn't fair at all and I was almost to the point where I was going to explode. For eight years I had put up with all of their bull shit and I was finally fed up. Yanking open the freezer I took out some steaks to thaw out for dinner tonight. Once that was sitting in cold water I went up to my room slamming the door behind me.

WHILE EVERYONE ATE THE LOVELY DINNER I MADE I STAYED in my room. Looking at the picture of my mom I picked it up and held it close to my heart. A lone tear fell down my face. I wished my mother was here. My father could have Angela and the girls, I didn't care. I just wanted my mother. I knew if she saw me now she wouldn't recognize me. I wasn't the outgoing, goofy little girl she left all those years ago. I was broken and I didn't know how to put myself back together again. Angela made sure to keep me from getting a job and experiencing the real world but I was going to make sure I got to live out my dreams. First I had to figure out how. My stomach growled letting me know it was time to eat. Getting out of bed I cracked my door open to listen out for the witches. The house was eerily quiet. Tiptoeing out of my room I went downstairs to get the plate I hid for myself. They always tried to make me eat bull shit while they ate lavishly. I cooked the shit I should be able to eat steak and lobster too. I loved a nice bowl of oodles and noodles but I liked steak too. Opening the pantry I took out the plate I hid earlier. It was still warm from the foil so I ran up to my room and started eating. I didn't want to heat it up and they come back and smell it. Then they would catch on to what I was doing. I ended up cutting a piece out of each of their steaks for myself. Just enough to fill me up and that they wouldn't miss it. The baked potato and cheese broccoli hit the spot also. After throwing my plate out I got in the bed. It was only nine but my day was over. Lost in my own thoughts I laid there staring out of the window at the moon.

The walls were beginning to close in on me and I couldn't escape. Why did my father have to meet Angela? I don't even get what he saw in her. Yea she was beautiful but her insides were ugly. I never understood why they hated me so much. I was only a little kid when I first met them. We used to play together, watch movies, and have sleepovers all the time before we moved in. I thought I was finally going to have sisters. Instead, they turned on me the moment my dad went back overseas. I went from being a part of the family to being their Cinderella. Except nobody was coming to rescue me from the evil stepsisters. I can remember that first night alone with them very clearly.

"I'm going to miss you so much Sparkle. You know that?" My father said to me.

"I'll miss you to daddy. Please come home soon."

"You know I can't princess but I'll be back in three months. But don't worry we'll talk all the time. Okay?"

"Okay." I pouted.

"Don't be sad. You have Angela and the girls. It'll be fun. Right?"

"Right." I smiled.

"Good. Now you be good for Angela. Don't give her a hard time and keep up with your schoolwork. You're a big girl now and you can help out around here."

"Yes I know. I can help cook and clean. I can pick out my own clothes for school and do my hair." I said proudly.

"My baby girl." My father beamed." Give me hug I have to go."

Hugging my father I held him tight. I was going to miss him but I knew being in the house with just girls would be so much fun. We could paint each other's nails and do facials. All the stuff I used to do with my mommy I could do with Angela. I was going to miss my father but I would be fine. I was too old to be crying and whining so I would suck it up. My father kissed me on my forehead before kissing Angela and the girl's goodbye. We sat on the porch and waved goodbye as he got in the car to head to the airport. Soon as the car disappeared Angela ushered us inside. Sitting us all down on the couch she paced in front of us. She turned to me and smiled. Smiling back at her I started to speak. I wanted to know what fun things we were going to do first. Before I could say anything the smile turned into a cold evil grin.

"For now on Sparkle you do as I say. Not following my direc-

tions will get your ass whooped. You will cook, clean, and help the girls with their homework. You will not join any after school programs. I want you home straight after school. No, you cannot have any friends over and under any circumstances, you are not allowed to use the phone unless your father calls. So don't go giving out our house number. Got it?"

"Not really." I shrugged.

"Okay." She sighed. "Let me put it like this. Your father isn't here and won't be here for a while. You will take care of me and my kids every need. If they want you to do their homework you do it. If I leave food out defrosting when I come home I expect a meal. It's not that hard don't act stupid." She huffed.

"I'm only twelve though I barely know how to cook."

"Figure it out. I got an old cookbook around here somewhere. The faster you learn the better for you. Now go up to your room me and the girls are going to watch a movie and eat ice cream."

"I want to watch a movie too," I whined.

"No, you don't you wanna go clean the bathroom."

"Why can't I watch a movie and eat ice cream too? I don't understand." I cried.

Angela stormed over to me and picked me up from my shirt. She swung me towards the stairs. Landing hard against the bottom stairs I cried even more. What was happening? Everything was fine ten minutes ago. Hearing giggles I wiped my tears and looked at Christiana and the twins. They were laughing at me while Angela just stood there waiting for me to get up. When I didn't get up fast enough she grabbed me again and pushed me. I slowly walked up the stairs and went to my bedroom to cry.

Life hasn't been the same since that day. Some days were better than others but most days I still hated it here. Thinking of that memory made me cry. I still felt like that little twelve-year-old girl getting her heart crushed by people who were supposed to love and take care of me. Closing my eyes I inhaled deeply. Tears stained my dingy pillows once again. I needed a miracle and fast.

Sipping my coffee I sat on my balcony reflecting on my life. A huge weight had been lifted off my shoulders but yet I still felt alone. The apartment was so quiet it scared me. By now London would be in the living room watching Maury or singing while she made eggs. Instead, it was just me all alone with my thoughts. I had to get out of here before I drove myself crazy. Getting up out of the chair I walked inside and locked the screen door behind me. I didn't know what I was going to do but I needed to do something. Picking up my keys and grabbing my phone I headed out the door. Didn't make sense to sit inside alone all day. After letting my car warm up a little I pulled out of my parking space with nowhere to go in mind. I turned up my radio and blasted some Jadakiss as I cruised the streets of Queens. Tyree's name popped up on my dashboard at the perfect time I needed moves.

"Yerrrrr." I chirped.

"Yerrrrrrr. What you fucking with my nigga?" he asked.

"Aint shit just driving around. What you and Jo fucking with. I need some moves."

"Jo out doing whatever it is she does and I'm out in L.I. right now. Had to go pick up some work. I'll be back around in a few hours. I gotta make a few stops before I head that way."

"Aight bet hit me my nigga I ain't doing shit."

"Aight I'll get at you in a few."

"Bet," I said and the phone disconnected.

If anyone could get me out of my slump it was Tyree. That nigga was a fool. Since I had a few more hours before we linked I headed to my grandma's house. Big momma always knew what I needed. I stopped by the lotto store on the corner and picked her up a few scratch-offs and a Smirnoff wine cooler. Pulling into the driveway I noticed my mom's car was there. Good, now I could get some love from the two most important people in my life. Using my key to let myself in I went straight to the back where I knew they would be. My mom and grandma were each sitting in a reclining chair watching Steve Wilkos.

"Hey, baby what you doing here?" MY mom asked standing up to hug me.

"Just came to see G-ma didn't expect to see you here."

"I came to drop off some shit and an hour later she got me watching Steve." She chuckled.

"Shhhh, We can talk when this goes off," Grandma mumbled.

I hugged and kissed her grandma before giving her her scratch-off and Smirnoff. She smiled back at me before turning her attention back to Steve. I knew how she felt about her shows so I sat quietly and watched the last fifteen minutes of the show with her. When it was over she got up and put the Smirnoff in the fridge and grabbed her cigarettes. Sitting back in the recliner she stared at me. My grandma always knew when something was off with me. She raised six kids and ten grandkids. I was the second oldest grandchild and growing up I spent a lot of time with her.

"What's wrong with you?"My Grandma asked.

"You slowing down old lady." I laughed."Took you long enough."

"Boy, you out your fucking mind. You know I can always tell when somethings wrong. Especially with you. Now did you get rid of that London broad yet?"

"Ma leave that girl alone. You know that boy loves her." My mom objected.

"What's love got to do with any damn thing? I don't like that girl it's something about her."

"Well, yea." My mom agreed." But you know Ry gets all sensitive and shit."

"No, I do not." I interrupted.

"What I tell you about lying? It's nothing wrong with it I just don't like that girl." Grandma continued.

"Well, it's over me and London broke up," I admitted.

"Good that little hoe was no good for you anyway."

"Ma." My mother snapped.

"But I am sorry." She added.

"What happened baby? Everything seemed fine a few weeks ago."

"She was cheating on me and stealing from me." I shrugged.

"See I knew it." My grandma confessed.

My mom and I cut our eyes at my grandma who slowly sunk into her chair. She raised her arms to surrender. Even back in high school, my grandma didn't like London. She always said she was sneaky but I never paid it any attention but I wished I had. I told them the story of how I found out. I could tell my grandmother wanted to say more but she kept her mouth shut. My mom was sympathetic, she didn't care for London either but she kept her disdain to herself. Which I greatly appreciated.

"How are you feeling since this all went down?" MY mom inquired.

"I'm fine momma I promise. I loved London but I haven't been in love with her for a while. I was more angry than hurt because she lied and stole from me but so many things started to make sense once she was gone."

"Okay if you're not fine that's okay too."

"I know but I'm good. She wasn't the one for me and I accepted that already."

"Some people come into your life for a reason and a season." My grandma spoke. " Some people are brought to you to teach you a lesson or show you the true path you're supposed to be on. So it may hurt and you may have your days when you dwell on it but baby I promise you those storms only last a little while before the sun comes back out."

"Amen." My mother cosigned.

"I know there's someone out there for me I'm not worried about that."

"Good, bring me home someone worth meeting please."

In my family, we always brought the person we were dating to meet my Grandmother before taking things to the next level. If they didn't get the stamp of approval they asses was out the door. My grandmother seemed to always be right when it came to these types of things. She had a sixth sense for smelling bull shit. Her stamp has saved people from a few heartaches.

"I will but please enough about that. I need your help with something else. I have this friend that's being abused by her family. They isolated her from the real world. She has no job, no money no work experience, nothing. I want to help her. I saw firsthand how she's living and it isn't right."

"If she has none of that how can you help?"

"I don't know I just feel like I have to do something. That shit makes me feel uneasy. She's so fragile and sweet. She doesn't deserve that her soul is too innocent."

"Sounds like you have a crush." My mom winked.

"It's nothing like that." I chuckled." I just met her a few weeks ago and I've only seen her like twice and the second time was on accident. Maybe I was meant to be there that night. I don't know.

"That doesn't mean shit. Those fate relationships are the strongest." My grandma answered.

"True." My mom agreed.

"When I met your grandfather it was an accident. I would never forget it. I was on my way to school and I forgot one of my books. I didn't really need it but I went back for it anyway. On the way back to school your grandfather was walking with one of his friends. I had never seen him before and didn't really pay him any mind. Well, I tripped and fractured my ankle and he and his friend helped me get back home. His friend left and he stayed with me until I could get to the doctor. We get to talking and he told me he had just moved to our town and he missed his ride so he had to walk. He said he was going to stay home but something kept nagging him to go to school so he did. And that's how we met and fell in love. We walked to school together every day after that and became inseparable. Two years later I got pregnant with your aunt and we packed up and moved to New York. I was barely eighteen but I was going to follow that man anywhere he went."

"Wow, I never knew that."

"I believe it was fate. If I wouldn't have left my books and he didn't miss his ride who knows if we would have ever crossed paths. Sometimes God will put you at the right place at the right time for the right reason."

"I agree with that but I don't know about all of that between Sparkle and I?"

"Her name is Sparkle? That's so cute." My mom cooed.

"I just want to help her but I don't know how. We barely know each other but my heart is telling me I need to do something. That night I ran into her by accident we talked for hours. She's unlike anyone I've ever met before. No matter what she's going through at home she still keeps a positive attitude and I really admire that."

"So this is what you do. Call her up and have her meet you somewhere, you bring her here and I'll talk to her. I'll call up some people and get her set up with a room and a job and whatever else she may need."

"She doesn't have a phone but I think I can help her with that too."

"I have a phone you can give her." My grandma replied getting up.

She walked into the kitchen and came back with a phone and the charger. Passing it to me I inspected it. It was in great condition. This would be perfect for Sparkle. Long as she could call or text me it was fine. Until we figured all of this out I wanted to be able to reach her so I could check on her each day.

"Thanks. This is perfect. Where did you get this from?"

"I gave it to her a few months ago and she never used it." My mom huffed.

"I told you the phone I have is fine and look it's getting used anyway so hush."

"Whatever mom. Anyway Ry it has unlimited talk and text plus internet."

"Great! I'm gonna go find her and give this to her. Hopefully, she doesn't get caught with it. I would hate to see what happens then."

Hugging my mom and grandma I got in my car and drove towards Sparke's house. I Didn't know how I was going to see her. If I had to just knock on the door then so be it. I hoped that wasn't the case though, I didn't want to get her in trouble. Pulling up to her block I parked a few houses down and shut the engine off. I didn't have to work today so I could sit here for a few and see if she shows her face. Plugging the phone into my car charger I programmed my phone number into it so she would have it. It had internet and she could download music if she wanted to.

For some reason I was nervous. My hands were sweaty and my heart was racing. It felt good doing something for someone. Especially when I know they would appreciate it. sitting outside for twenty minutes the door to the house finally opened. Four ladies walked out and got in the car and left. I waited a few minutes before pulling up in front of the house.

I LAID OUT ON THE COUCH IN MY PAJAMAS WATCHING A movie. It was late afternoon and after sleeping in I was kind of bored. My thoughts kept drifting to O'Rion even though I didn't want to. One of the most embarrassing nights of my life ended up turning around. Talking to O'Rion for hours gave me a boost in my confidence. He was so confident in the way he spoke and the way he carried himself. Something I wished I had. All I needed was someone to talk to. The way I was living my life wasn't good for me in the long run. I had to do something and I needed to do it quick. I just didn't know how. I could ask my father for money but then again Angela always stood there when I talked to him just to make sure I didn't say anything. He had plans to come home in a few months so maybe I could wait til then I thought. When he was home he would come up and spend time with just me for a little. Then I could make my move. I always looked forward to it but as I got older and the treatment from Angela and Christiana got worse I just stopped caring if he even came home. I just didn't understand why he changed and it hurt. This time I couldn't wait for him to come home, it was my last chance. The doorbell rang interrupting my quiet time. Groaning I got off the couch to answer the door. I had no idea who it could be. The girls didn't tell me they were expecting a package so I was clueless. I looked through the peephole and smiled. Opening the door I unlocked it and closed it behind me.

"Hey O'Rion what are you doing here?" I asked checking my surroundings.

"I uh honestly couldn't stop thinking about you and just wanted to make sure you were ok."

"I'm fine thanks for asking." I blushed." How are you?"

"I'm good, I was in the neighborhood and thought I'd pass by. Is anyone home?"

"No, they're all gone I finally have some peace and quiet." I nervously laughed.

"Good. You deserve it."

"Thanks. I-I wanted to thank you for the other night. You don't know how much that meant to me and how much it changed things. I just want you to know how much I appreciate it."

"Don't mention it Sparkle. It was the least I could do."

"But you didn't have too and that means everything." I smiled.

He smiled back at me and time stood still. His deep dimples and smile were electrifying. I had this feeling in the pit of my stomach and I didn't know what it meant but it made my insides all warm and fuzzy.

"Uhh, I got something for you." He stated snapping me out of my thoughts. "Here."

Opening the brown paper bag I looked inside and found a cell phone and charger. I'd never had a cell phone before. Thoughts of everything I could do flooded my brain instantly.

"Wow. I don't know what to say. Thank you O'Rion. "

"You're welcome Sparkle. Now we can talk whenever and it'll be easier to help you this way."

"This is crazy. Are you like my guardian angel or something." I said as a tear fell from my eye.

"Please don't cry." He whispered.

"I'm sorry it's just I've never had a phone before and here you are just giving it to me. I don't know what I did to deserve this."

"You deserve the best of the best Sparkle and once we get you out of here you'll have everything your heart desires."

"My heart desires to get out of here anything else is just extra. Thank you again. You don't know me from a hole in the wall but here you are helping me. Why?"

"I didn't like seeing that shit the other day, It honestly broke my heart to see you being treated like that. I could tell the day in Jim's that you were broken but I didn't know why and now I see. I also see how pure your heart is and someone as pure as you doesn't need to be tainted by heartless souls. You're so much better than these people and if it's the last thing I do I'm going to get you out of here. Okay?"

"Okay." I nodded.

"Good. Its cold out here so go inside and play around with your phone. I already programmed my number so you can call or text me whenever. Don't hesitate to reach out if you need me."

"I won't and thank you again. This can literally change my life and I'm forever grateful."

He reached his hand out and pulled me in for a hug. His cologne filled my nostrils making my knees weak. It was different from before but it stilled smelled good. He pulled away and kissed me on my forehead before he jogged down the steps and got into his car. I waited until he pulled off before going inside. Closing the door, I finally let out that breath I had been holding in. It was freezing out but my body was on fire. I ran upstairs to my room and hid the phone under my mattress. I didn't need them finding that. Since it was getting later in the day I decided to clean up the house before the girls got home. They were always quick to snitch and call Angela and I didn't want to give them a reason to. I turned to a music channel and turned it up just enough so I could hear it as I cleaned the house. I twirled and danced around the house as I cleaned. Having the house to myself and seeing O'Rion put a smile on my face. Plus I finally had a phone I was on top of the world. I was going to clean up the house and lock myself in my room while I figured out how to work it. I didn't know why O'Rion wanted to help me. Didn't you help people that you liked? it's not like he thought I was attractive or anything like that so I couldn't understand. Then again I had no experience with men so I don't know what they really thought. One half of me was fighting with the idea that he was being so nice. I just didn't get it. The other half of me was telling the other to shut the fuck up and enjoy it so I can get the fcuk outta here.

"Sparkle where yo ass at?" I heard from the kitchen.

"I'm in the kitchen," I yelled back.

Christiana cut the music off and stormed into the kitchen. Her nostrils flared and all I could see was Angela in her. I guess that's where she got that stupid shit from.

"What do you think you're doing?"

"Umm washing the dishes." I retorted.

"I can see that you idiot. I mean with the TV?"

"Well, you guys weren't here so I figured I could enjoy it." I shrugged.

"Don't touch shit that doesn't belong to you." She screamed.

"It don't belong to you either," I mumbled.

"What the fuck did you say?" She said through gritted teeth.

"I SAID IT DON'T BELONG TO YOU EITHER."

"Oh okay, little bitch think she cute. Cool, I got something for you. Ava and Asia will be here soon." She smiled then turned to walk away.

Nothing could bring me down from my high right now. Not even Chris and her funky ass attitude. I finished washing the dishes and then started mopping the floor. Fifteen minutes later Asia and Ava got home. When Christiana heard them come in she rushed downstairs. I could hear them talking I just didn't know what they were saying. Next thing I knew they were all surrounding me in the kitchen.

"So what was all that fly shit you were talking a little while ago?" Christiana asked.

"You know what I said Chris. I don't know why you went to go get your little minions." I said continuing to mop.

"Who the fuck got you felling yourself?" Ava asked.

"I'm just tired of yal shit. Okay? Ava and Asia only act like a bitch because you do. I never did anything to yal." I said throwing the mop down to the floor." NOTHING! All you guys do is fuck with me and I'm over it."

"First of all." Christian began.

"No fuck that." I said waving her off." You think you're better than me but you're not. You're a miserable ass bitch with nothing going for herself besides trying to trap her boyfriend with a baby. Congrats you're such a fucking winner." I sneered. "And Ava if you would get out Chris' ass for a second you would see that she's been stealing money from you but you're so concerned about me. Asia, you're nice to me when Chris isn't around and I appreciate it and all but just be you and stop trying to be a kiss ass like your sister. You're so much better than all of them. Angela too." I shrugged.

It felt so good to get that off my chest. I had been holding that in for years. It was so much more shit that I could say that would have the three of them fighting each other right now. They were so crazy and it was ridiculous. They would be mean to me and give me their ass to kiss but if they needed someone to listen to their stories I was the first one they came to. When Christiana had that pregnancy scare last year she came to me first not her beloved sisters. I was way too nice and they didn't deserve it. I had a good heart and that was probably my biggest downfall. I didn't have a mean bone in my body at this point I was just so fed up with their shit. I should expose all their secret conversations about each other and sit back and watch them kill each other.

"Bitch." Ava gritted getting in my face." You better watch your fucking mouth."

"Or what you're gonna tell your mommy?" I said mocking her.

From the corner of my eye, I saw Asia laugh. Which brought a smile to my face. Right then and there I realized I had no reason to be scared of them. They were a bunch of big ass babies with nothing going for themselves. The only reason they acted like this is because their mom trained them to when we were younger.

"See even your twin thinks you're a big baby."

"The fuck you laughing at?" Ava snapped her head around and yelled.

"It was funny." She shrugged.

"Wanna know what else is funny? Christiana fucked Cole that's why he left you." I smiled. 'But wait there's more. She got pregnant and he made her get an abortion. Oops did I say that?" I giggled.

"You bitch!" Ava Screamed charging Christiana.

Ava got all in her face yelling and screaming. I sat back for a while and watched them go at it. Somehow Asia got involved and now the three of them were arguing back and forth. I walked away and went upstairs. I spun around my room as If I was floating because that's how I felt. Who knew sticking up for yourself would make you feel this good. I knew I would get in trouble once Angela came home and they told her but I didn't care anymore. Being locked in my room is what I wanted anyway. At least ill be able to play on my new phone in peace. Sitting in bed I pulled the phone out and texted O'Rion.

Me: Hey its Sparkle

O'Rion: I know lol I saved your number

Me: Oh Sorry I should have known

O'rion: We gotta get you to stop apologizing how you feeling tho

Me: I just told them about themselves I feel good actually

O'Rion: Are you ok?

Me: Never been better

O'Rion: Good

They would have to find their own dinner cuz I'm not cooking shit for them. For the rest of the night, I stayed in my room with the door locked texting O'Rion. I could hear them still arguing an hour later and all I could do was laugh.Little did they know all of our lives were about to change. Some for the better and some for the worse. As O'rion and I texted I went through the phone trying to learn how to work it. I decided to try searching for my mom. Finding her was my main goal. If I could find her maybe I could go and live with her. I tried googling her name but nothing came up. I tried a bunch of different combinations until some articles popped. I read them over taking in all this new info. It wasn't much but the little information that was there told me things I had never known. She was charged with vehicular manslaughter in the second degree and endangering the welfare of a child. For all these years I never knew all the details. When I asked her she would always change the subject and then the phone call would end shortly after. Same thing with my father, after a while I just stopped asking. In the back of my mind, I always wondered and now I had some answers.

I wanted to find her so I could write her. I had hope that when she got out I could go with her. In my mind, I could deal with living with these evil witches if I knew I would have a new start with her. I was beginning to lose hope until O'rion suggested I do a NY inmate search. When her name popped up on the site I thanked O'rion again for being my guardian angel. As I kept looking I found out she was released last year and my heart sunk. In my heart, I knew I would never find her now but I tried to remain positive. I had to it was the only hope I had. For the rest of the night O'rion and I texted back and forth while I continued my search. I still had a lot of questions but my main concern was to find her. I had lost a lot of faith but I would always keep searching.

O'RION

The last of the leaves were falling off the tree and Winter was creeping up on us slowly. My life had changed drastically over these past few weeks just like the weather. After my breakup, things were rocky at first. I was having trouble remembering the things I enjoyed doing. Now I found myself smiling more and doing things I really wanted to do. After meeting with Sparkle I was going to take a bartending class tonight. I worked the clubs doing security might as well find other sources of income, you could never have too much money. Getting out the car I walked into the supermarket. Sparkle was waiting for me right by the front door. The only way we could see each other was when she had to run errands for the people who were supposed to be her family.

"Hey." She smiled." Thanks for meeting me."

"It's my pleasure. I need to do some grocery shopping myself so kill two birds with one stone."

"Cool. So how was your day?" she asked as we began walking through the store.

" went to work earlier and then went to the gym for a little and now I'm here with you. I'd say that was a pretty good day."

Sparkle blushed but didn't say anything as she picked up some ground beef. I don't know what compelled me to say it but it was true. I was enjoying Sparkle's company. We mostly talked on the phone and texted but that was more than enough for now. Once she was in a better situation things would be a lot different. The past few weeks I had gotten to know a lot about her and her about me. I hated the way her family treated her. I would hear them yelling in the background sometimes and she always came back to the phone different. Her attitude, her mindset everything was different. It sucked because she was amazing but her family brought her down. We were still trying to figure out how I could help. We hadn't come up with much but I wouldn't stop until she was far away from them.

'I need to get stuff to make Lasagna. That's what they want for dinner tonight."

"I hate Lasagna."

"Me too. After eating it so much I can't stand it. That's all they want though either that or Spaghetti."

"it's basically the same thing."

"I know that's what I say but they claim it's not. They will eat that five to six times a month."

"Nah that's too much."

"I don't eat it anymore. At this point, I go hungry or find some crackers to munch on."

"That's not good Sparkle. You gotta eat better than that."

" I know but I don't get a say in what we eat. I just cook it."

"Well, what's your favorite foods?

"I love tacos and making homemade pizzas oh and peanut butter. Love me some peanut butter." She laughed." I used to do those with my mom all the time. we would make homemade pizzas on Fridays and have taco Tuesdays. Sometimes we would sit on the couch with a jar of peanut butter and just dig in with our spoons. "

"I still do that." I laughed.

"Me too. I keep a jar in my room that nobody knows about. It helps me survive."

"You shouldn't have to survive, you should be living."

"I know I know but I have a feeling ill get there soon." She smiled.

Sparkle and I walked around the store getting everything we needed. I made her get a few items for herself that she could keep in her room undetected. She wasn't eating right, cups of noodles and scraps of food wouldn't cut it anymore. Not with me around at least. She was hesitant to let me pay for her food but she really had no choice. I wouldn't take no for an answer. I told her to keep the money and save it. in her situation you never knew when you would need some money. Packing the groceries in my car we headed back towards Sparkle's place so I could drop her off and get to my bartending class. Pulling over a block away from her house I put the car in park. I couldn't let her out near her place I didn't want her to get in trouble.

"Thanks for coming with me O'rion and thanks again for the food."

"Don't mention it, we can do this once a week. Plus it gives you more you time once you don't have to wait on the bus."

"I would love that. I know you have to go and so do I. Text me after your class is over."

"I will have a good rest of the day Sparkle."

"You too O'rion."

Getting out of the car Sparkle grabbed her bags and walked off towards her house. I followed slowly behind her to make sure she got there safe. It was only five but it was getting darker outside earlier. Once she made it to her door she quickly waved before disappearing inside the house. I headed home so I could put up my food and relax for a bit. My bartending class didn't start until seven so I had plenty of time. Jolie and Tyree wanted to try it so they were going to meet me there. I was always the third wheel so I didn't mind. Jolie wanted to beat London up every time she saw her so we usually didn't do things together. I was happy to be taking this class. I wish Sparkle could come it would be fun and it's a possible source of income. Pulling into my apartment complex I got out and headed inside.

Tyree, Jolie, and I had fun at our first bartending class. We sat around talking with the owner for a while. The class was fun and entertaining and she even offers job placement after you obtain your bartending license. I was glad I came trying new things that were on my list for the upcoming year. Grabbing our drinks we sat down at a table nearby.

"Thanks for inviting us bro. This shit was lit."

"No doubt."

"We should have a party to show off our skills." Jolie blurted out.

"Baby I don't think we on that level yet."

"Well, when we get there we can. We can make specialty drinks and have a contest to see who has the best drink."

"Oh, you already know imma beat that ass," Tyree replied.

"Yea whatever." She waved him off." Ry how you been?"

"I'm cool Jo." I shrugged." Working and shit."

"You been kinda distant lately. You sure you good?"

"Yea I'm sure. I just been adjusting to the single life. That's why I'm here, to be honest. I can finally do the things I want to do."

"That's great. I know it's a big adjustment but it'll be fine in the end."

"I'm not worried about it. I can finally focus on myself more. I've been kind of helping someone out so that keeps me going too."

"What do you mean you've been helping someone? Someone like who?"

"Her name is Sparkle-"

"Her?" Tyree said.

"Yes her. I met her a few weeks back the day me and London broke up. Remember that girl who got slapped over the cupcakes?"

"Yea."

"it's her."

"Oh my god."

"Her stepsisters are the ones who through the party."

"I didn't like that shit at all."

"Yea that was fucked up. It wasn't even that serious." Tyree agreed.

"I would have whooped everyone ass that night."

"They treat her like shit Jo. That's why I'm helping her. I don't like that shit either and I feel bad. She's one of the nicest, sweetest people I have ever met."

"I get it Ry but you can't save everyone and I don't want you to get hurt. Look what happened with London. You tried to save her and that backfired."

"I know but she's nothing like London. She's not like anyone I've met before. Plus I'm not trying to date her I just want to help her. They abuse her and that shit don't sit well with me."

"Aww, I feel you. You know I'm overprotective over you and Ty."

"I know sis and I appreciate it. I just couldn't sit by and watch her get treated like that."

"I know Ava and Asia we go to the same nail salon and we became cool. I didn't know they were giving it up like that though."

"From what she tells me it's the other sister that does most of the bullying. The twins just follow."

"Ugh, I hate following ass bitches." Jolie spat.

"I don't really know what to do though. I got her a phone so we can communicate but I'm struggling with what's next. She has no job experience which can be solved but where will she live? It's so much to figure out."

"Yea it is a lot but me and Ty will help however we can. Right baby?"

"Well since you volunteered." He scoffed." But nah my nigga I got you."

"Aight bet."

We stayed there for another hour before heading home. The night was still young but I didn't have any other plans. Walking into my apartment I kicked off my shoes at the door and collapsed on the couch. As I started to doze off my front door opened. Looking up London was standing there with a plastic bag that was filled with clothes.

"Oh, I didn't think you would be here."

"Why not it is my apartment. My question is what are you doing here?"

"Me and Key got into an argument so I came here."

"Okay but why? You and I are NOT friends. I don't under-stand why you insist on trying."

"Ry-"

"Nah Ry my fucking ass," I replied getting off the couch.

"What don't you understand London? Huh? Do you enjoy pissing me off? Do you get your rocks off by fucking with my life?"

"I'm not here for that, I'm here cuz I needed a place to go for a few hours. Maybe take a shower and hang like we used to."

"I DON'T WANT TO HANG WITH YOU!"I screamed. "Are you fucking stupid or slow or both?"

"Calm down O'rion." She snapped." You weren't perfect in the relationship. Your actions caused all of this."

"My actions? Really? If you didn't want to be with me all you had to do was leave. Not lie, cheat, and steal. Are you Eddie Guerrero or something? You ruined this relationship with your selfish actions. I didn't want much from you just to be honest and real with me. I let you live with me, I took care of your every need. Mentally, physically and emotionally and you couldn't even give me half of that. "

"I cheated because you wouldn't marry me. ALL YOU HAD TO DO WAS MARRY ME." She cried

"And you still would have cheated. You weren't worth marrying because all you care about is yourself. Look at you, these little baby tears don't mean anything to me. Save that shit for someone else. Leave my key and get the fuck out of my apartment. You got some fucking nerve."

"I didn't come here to argue with you. We were friends before anything, be my friend, please Ry."

Looking at her I felt nothing. I didn't care she was crying, I didn't care that her and her girlfriend got into it. None of that was my problem. People like London never learned. They just found new ways to get what they wanted out of people. Then they would move on to their next victim. All along I was just another notch under her belt. She saw me as her meal ticket. She never really loved me and I wish I saw all of that before I fell back in love with her and moved her in. I wish I knew that before I upgraded her life. But I didn't and I would have to live with that. While she had to live with the fact that she lost the best thing that would ever happen to her.

"Get out." I gritted.

"Ry." She whispered.

"Get the fuck out London," I yelled.

Spit flew out my mouth and my chest rose up and down. I was starting to see red. London jumped at the tone of my voice and scurried out the door. I was changing my locks in the morning. Thank god I never put her on my lease. Rubbing my hands down my face I sighed and sat back down. My heart was racing, I was pissed the fuck off. I needed to release some steam. Getting off the couch I ran into my room and put on some basketball shorts and a T-shirt. My building had a gym downstairs, I was going to work out until the anger inside of me went away. Grabbing my phone and keys I locked up and walked to the elevator. My phone vibrated in my hands letting me know I had a text.

Sparkle: How was your class?

Just seeing her name calmed me down slightly. I could picture her so vividly in my head, smiling and laughing. If it was up to me I would be on my way to see Sparkle right now. Opening up the text I replied and headed down to the gym. It was empty when I get here which I liked. I went straight for the punching bag. I needed to let out all of this frustration and since I didn't want to be in London's presence and take it out on her I would take it out on the bag.

EVER SINCE I FOUND OUT MY MOM HAD BEEN RELEASED I HAD been in a slump. I couldn't shake the feeling I would never see her again. I had always held out hope that she would find me but now things just seemed impossible. With Christmas coming up in a few days I was really starting to get sad. This was one of the worst parts of being in this family. Not only did I never get gifts or even a merry Christmas but since I was fifteen I stayed home alone while they went away. Over the years I've gotten used to it but I still wished I had a family or someone to spend the day with. Every year Angela would tell my father I was being bad around this time to cover her tracks on why I wasn't around or the fact I didn't get any gifts. Even at twenty, she would tell him she sent me to my room because I threw a tantrum and cried myself to sleep. He never questioned it but I questioned it all the time.

Angela had left me to pack all of their clothes for the trip while she went out to go hoe or whatever it was she did throughout the day. The girls were gone and I was happy to have some peace. The days leading up to Christmas things always seem to get worse around here and I couldn't wait for them to leave tonight. I planned on laying on the couch watching movies and eating anything I want. I finished packing their bags then went to my room to relax. In a few hours, the house will be mine. Pulling out my phone from under my mattress I saw I had messages from O'rion. Smiling I unlocked the phone and texted him back. The last few days his mood was off. He said everything was ok but I could tell it wasn't. I didn't want to stress him with my problems so I kept them so myself. Hopefully, he would open up to me and tell me what was wrong. Even now the conversation seemed different but I wanted him to know I was there for him so I didn't say anything.

Ry: My break is over but ill talk to you when I get off

Me: okay they just got home but we can talk on the phone tonight

Ry: Can't wait talk to you later.

Me: Enjoy the rest of your day

Sliding the phone back under the mattress I laid down waiting for them to come and find me. It only took three minutes before Angela barged into my room.

"You finished packing already? She asked.

"Yes just finished five minutes ago."

"Good now clean out the trunk and put our bags in. I was nice enough to buy you a few groceries while we're gone. If you eat it all that's on your dumbass. Put the groceries up then go do the trunk."

I didn't say anything and she didn't give me a chance to she just slammed the door and walked away. As I walked down the stairs I wondered what she had gotten me. That was actually kind of nice of her. Usually, she brought a box noodles and I lived off of that and whatever little shit was in the house. They thought I didn't realize but they always ate up all the food so there was nothing for me to even make. No eggs, no cheese no bread nothing.

Walking into the kitchen I saw two bags on the table. There was a loaf of bread, six cans of Vienna sausages, crackers, and some corn beef hash. I was happy about the bread and corned beef but Vienna sausages. Really? In the other bag was a whole bunch of noodles. Of course, she couldn't forget the damn noodles. Thankfully I still had the stuff Ry brought for me to keep in my room. I still had the money to so I would be fine either way. After I put the groceries away I grabbed my coat and went outside to clean out the trunk. Of course, it was nasty as hell. There were old McDonald's wrappers and shit stuck to the carpet.

"Hey Sparkle," Asia said.

"Hey," I replied dryly.

"I know Christmas is hard for you so I umm got you something. I can't give it to you now but ill leave it in my room under my pillow."

"Oh wow thank you."

"Asia get in here. Why are you talking to the help?" Christiana yelled.

"Bye Sparkle." She whispered.

Scurrying away she disappeared into the house. Only a few more hours and they would be gone I told myself. Opening up the garbage back I brought out with me I throughout all the garbage in the trunk and then brought out there suitcases and put them in. My fingertips were freezing so I went inside to warm up once I was done. Everyone was sitting around talking and laughing but when I walked in they got quiet. Ignoring them I began to make my way to my room but Angela stopped me.

"Took you long enough. "She spat.

"It was a lot of garbage." I shrugged.

"Don't get smart. We're leaving soon so I wanted to go over the rules again."

"I know the rules. Don't leave the house, don't go in our rooms, and don't have anyone in the house even though I don't have friends."

"It's almost Christmas and I'm in a good mood so I'll let your smart ass comments go. For now. Let's call your father so you can tell him what you did and why you're not going again."

"Well, what's the excuse this year?"

"I don't know make something up I don't care."

"Fine."

Pulling out her phone Angela dialed up his number and put it on speaker. I wanted to get this over with so they can leave me alone. Each day that went by the less I cared. I was just trying to survive until O'rion and I figured something out. That was the only thing I was worried about.

"Hey Honey." He said.

"Hey baby we're getting ready to leave but Sparkle needs to tell you something."

"Hey father," I said as she passed me the phone.

"Hey baby girl, what's up?"

"Well umm I'm not going to Mt. Vernon this year. I uhh have really bad cramps and just don't feel good."

"Aww, baby girl take some Advil and feel better. You should really try to go. It's Christmas."

"Yea I know but I don't want to be moody you know how I get."

"True." He laughed." Well, ill talk to you soon. Merry Christmas and I love you."

"Yea love you too," I replied. "Bye."

"Bye." He said hanging up.

"Really dumbass? That's all you can come up with?" Christiana said.

"You really trying me little bitch. Get out my face." Angela spat.

Turning around I laughed to myself. I thought it was funny plus if they wanted me to lie they could have at least came up with the lie themselves. Closing my bedroom door I laid in bed staring at the ceiling. I could see from my window them getting in the car and leaving. I waited ten minutes just in case they had to come back for something. Walking into the twin's room I looked under Asia's pillow to find fifty dollars and a note.

Order yourself something nice for Christmas dinner.

Merry Christmas

-Asia

That was really sweet of her. I thought there might've been a catch so I kept the note just in case. I was going to save the money instead of ordering food. It would come in handy later on down the line. The night was still young but I was tired. After making me some corn beef hash and grits I showered and laid on the couch watching Home Alone and eating sugar cookies I had made. Around nine O'rion texted me to let me know he was home and I could call whenever I wanted. I had nothing else to do so I called him immediately.

Waking up this morning I felt sad. Usually on Christmas London would attempt to make breakfast and I would act like I enjoyed it. Then we would sit and open gifts before heading out for the day. Instead, I woke up to A Christmas Story playing and no food being made. Getting out of bed I went to the bathroom to take care of my hygiene. Then I texted Sparkle. Walking into my kitchen I looked through my fridge for breakfast. Deciding on eggs, grits, and corn beef hash I started cooking. My phone vibrated in my pocket. When I pulled it out it was Sparkle.

"Merry Christmas." I sung into the phone.

"Merry Christmas O'Rion."

"How are you today?"

"I'm great, everyone is gone for the rest of the week."

"Wait, So you're spending Christmas by yourself?"

"Yup. I do every year. They always go up to Mt. Vernon to my stepmother's Grandparents."

"When do they come back?"

"She said Sunday night."

"Perfect. You're coming out with me."

"Wait. Where are we going?"

"My grandma lives not too far from you. That's where we are spending Christmas."

"Wow thank you for the invite but I don't know O'Rion."

"You don't have a choice. You're NOT spending the day alone. Okay?"

"Fine. What time?"

"Like three I'll be there to pick you up."

"Okay great. I have time to make cupcakes or something."

"You don't have to bring anything just come and enjoy some good eats."

"I have to bring something. You never go to someone's house empty-handed. My mom always taught me that."

"True. What else can you bake?" I asked trying to make conversation.

"Umm Cakes, and brownies. Cookies are my favorite thing to bake. I want to try cheesecake but I've never had a reason too. I usually bake when Angela or the girls need me too."

"I love cheesecake. Specially Juniors."

"Me too. I've only had juniors once like ten years ago but I remember it was the best cheesecake I had ever tasted."

"Maybe we can go one day."

"I would love that." She replied.

I could feel her blushing through the phone. I was too, I didn't understand why but I always did when we spoke. She was so funny and I don't think she realized it. It's sad what her family was doing to her. Because of them she couldn't live up to her full potential and she had the potential to go far.

"I'm glad. I gotta get this breakfast started I'll call you when I'm on my way."

"Okay see you later. Bye." She replied hanging up.

Smiling at the phone I put it down and got my breakfast

started. I still had a lot to do today. I still hadn't wrapped my gifts. I'm just glad we do secret Santa in my family because I didn't have time to buy gifts for everybody and their mother. I got my mom, grandma, my cousin Tyree and Jolie a gift plus my secret Santa which was my fifteen-year-old cousin Yasmin. Once those were wrapped and I ate I could chill out for the next few hours until it was time to pick up Sparkle. I don't know why my dumbass didn't get her a gift. I could imagine what Christmas was like for her over the years so I knew a gift would probably put a smile on her face. While my corn beef baked in the oven I went into my spare room to see if I had any stuff laying around I could put together for her. I rummaged through the room and found a few of London's stuff still with the tags on it. She probably wouldn't be back to get it so Sparkle could enjoy it. Plus it was still in the Nordstrom bag I brought it home in. I was so glad her ungrateful ass wasn't in my life anymore.

Bringing the stuff into the living room I went through the bag to see what was in there. London and Sparkle were the same height. Sparkle was thicker and had a lot more curves but everything should fit. I found four sweaters, two pairs of jeans and an Ugg hat and scarf set. I found a gift bag to put it in and put it with the rest of my gifts, By the time I finished that it was time to eat and relax.

I was on my way to pick up Sparkle. I was nervous as hell, I hoped she liked her gift. I started second-guessing my gift but Jolie said it was okay to give Sparkle London's unwanted and unused stuff. It felt weird but Jolie reassured me. That calmed me a lot but now I'm in the car and on my way to pick her up I couldn't get the knot out of my stomach. Pulling up to her house I grabbed the bag and went to go knock on the door. When she opened the door it took my breath away. The way she was glowing tightened the knot in my stomach. Whatever perfume she was wearing I could smell it soon as she opened the door. it was light and fruity.

"Merry Christmas. Again." She laughed.

"Merry Christmas Sparkle," I said pulling her into a hug.

"I'm ready." She replied as I let her go." I just need to get the cupcakes. Come in."

Nervously I looked around to make sure nobody was watching. Even though I knew her people were gone you never knew who was watching. Stepping inside I closed the door behind me. Sparkle disappeared into the kitchen and came back shortly with a pan of cupcakes.

"Look." She said lifting up the foil.

They were chocolate cupcakes decorated with Tree-shaped sprinkles. They looked and smelled amazing I couldn't wait to try them.

"Those look great Sparkle I kind of want one now."

"Well you can't have any now but after dinner, you can have as many as you'd like." She smiled.

"Okay, mom I won't spoil dinner." I joked.

"Good boy." She laughed.

"Before I forget I got you something," I said handing her the gift bag.

"Wow, O'Rion you didn't have to do that. I feel bad I didn't get you anything." She pouted.

"Seeing you smile is more than enough."

That was so corny I thought to myself. It was true though I loved seeing her eyes light up when she smiled. It lit up the whole room. It made me feel at peace seeing her happy. I watched her closely as she looked at each item. Tears welled up in her eyes, I hope I didn't offend her.

"What's wrong Sparkle? Why are you crying?"

"I love everything." She sniffled." I just been wondering lately why?"

"Why what?"

"Why are you so nice to me?"

"I'm just a nice person Sparkle, most people are. I know it's hard to believe with the hand you've been dealt but there are people out there who care about you."

"Do you care about me?" she asked.

Hearing her ask me that broke my heart but the look in her eyes made me feel even worse. Here this girl was craving love and affection and she had nowhere to get it from. I hadn't known her that long but I cared very deeply for her and I hoped she believed me.

"Of course I do."

"I believe you. It's just sometimes I really wonder what I did to deserve this? I'm just Sparkle, there's nothing special about me but yet every time we talk I feel like the only person in the world."

"I don't want to hear you say that Ever again." I snapped.

When she jumped I felt horrible. I had to remember she had been through a lot and was fragile as hell. Yelling was obviously a trigger for her.

"I didn't mean to yell Spark. I just don't want you talking like that about yourself. You are something special and I know it may not seem like it but you are. You hear me?"

"Yes. "she nodded.

"Good, now let's go eat."

"Okay, but can I change real quick. I look horrible and now that I have new clothes I want to look good for your family."

"Sure. I'll wait right here." I smiled.

While she changed I looked around the house. There were pictures of the stepmom and her girls but not one picture of Sparkle. I couldn't understand why they hated her so much. To me, Sparkle was kind, sweet and funny. Some people were just naturally mean and miserable I guess. Sitting back down on the couch I waited for Sparkle to come back down. When she did she was smiling from ear to ear. I could see in her eyes how happy she was and that made me happy. The red Ralph Lauren sweater looked perfect on her. Along with the new jeans she just got. They hugged her thighs just right showing off her curvy body.

"So how do I look?" she asked as she spun around.

"You look amazing. How does everything fit?"

"Like a glove. I'm not used to such good materials but it feels great on my skin. Usually, I just wear leggings and sweaters that I knit myself." She shrugged. "I feel great though thank you again."

"You're welcome. You ready to go, I'm starving."

"Me too. Let's go."

I grabbed the pan of cupcakes while Sparkle put on her coat and made sure she had everything. I followed her out of the house and waited while she locked up. Putting the cupcakes in the back seat I opened the door then ran to the driver's side and pulled off. Sparkle and I drove quietly the few blocks to my grandma's house. I could feel the nervousness radiating off of her.

"You nervous?"

"Is it that obvious?" She laughed.

"Yes, and it's ok I know a lot of this is new to you but as long as I'm here we'll get through it together."

"Okay. I'm calm. Is there anything I need to know before we go in there?"

"Umm not really. My uncles might crack jokes but its harmless. Other than that just enjoy the good eats." I replied pulling into the driveway.

Getting out of the car I grabbed the cupcakes and Sparkle followed me inside. Soon as the door opened my stomach growled. I couldn't wait to eat. Everyone was sitting in the backroom watching A Christmas Story and drinking. My crazy uncle Ed was the first to notice me.

"Wassup Nephew." He screamed across the room.

"Wassup unc? Hey everybody, this is my friend Sparkle. Sparkle this is everyone."

"Hey Sparkle." Some of my aunts said in unison.

"Hi." She waved.

"Come in. Take your coat off and get comfortable." My mom said.

My mom walked over to us and took our coats and then came back for the cupcakes. She peeled back the foil and smiled. My mom was happy to meet Sparkle. When I called and asked if I could bring her she was ecstatic. I just hoped she didn't pull out the baby books and start showing my baby pictures.

"These look great Sparkle."

"Thank you ma'am."

"Please call me Olivia. Would you like something to drink? We have soda, water, beer whatever you like." She replied pointing to the cooler full of drinks.

"Umm ill have Dr. Pepper."

"You like that stuff too? We only by it cuz O likes it."

"It's my favorite soda." She smiled." Most people hate it but I love it. I never met someone else who likes it."

"I'll take one too momma."

"Okay baby."

While my mom got our sodas I found somewhere for me and Sparkle to sit. There were people everywhere but I found a spot right by the dining room table. When it was time to eat Sparkle and I would be the first ones there before the savages got to it.

Sparkle sat close to me taking in everything. I could tell she hadn't been around people like my folks before. She didn't look scared just intrigued.

"Here you go baby." My mom said passing us the soda.

"Thank you." Sparkle replied.

"Where Grandma? I want to introduce her to Sparkle."

"She's downstairs doing something. I don't know but soon as she comes up we'll heat up the food then we can eat."

"Good, I'm starving."

"You always starving." My grandma said emerging from the basement.

"I can't help it ma you know I love your cooking."

"I know baby."

" I wanna introduce you to Sparkle."

"Hi, it's nice to meet you." Sparkle smiled.

"You too my dear, I've heard a lot about you." She smirked.

"Well, that makes me nervous." She laughed.

"Don't be my grandson speaks very highly of you."

Sparkle smiled at me and I could see the sparkle in her eyes. I could only imagine how good it made her feel knowing someone spoke positively about her. This is how I wanted her to feel every day. I truly wished I had the power to make her feel like this all the time. I wish I had the power to take away her pain.

"That makes my heart smile. Not too many people speak so highly of me."

"Fuck em sweetie. If my grandson says your good people then you're good people. Now let's get this food heated up so the heathens can eat." She replied making us laugh. "Ry can you go get them bags and bring them up for me?"

"Sparkle will you be okay while I run downstairs real quick."

"Boy if you don't go on. What the hell you think we going to do to her in three minutes." My grandma snapped.

"I'll be fine." She giggled.

I looked back at Sparkle to get some reassurance she would be ok before disappearing down the stairs. She didn't have much interaction with people besides her family so I just wanted to make sure she was comfortable. I remember how she was when I first met her at the cleaners. She had come a long way in the past few weeks. She was still very shy and timid but when she was talking to me all her fears and anxieties went away. Grabbing bag of gifts I brought them upstairs. Sparkle was sitting at the kitchen table with my mom, my two aunts, and my little cousin Sasha. She seemed to be enjoying herself and that put me at ease.

"She's fine O'Rion stop staring." My mom stated.

"Ma!" I said cutting my eyes at her.

"What?" She shrugged." Calm down, isn't it time for you and your cousins to go for a walk." She winked.

"You crazy ma but no."

"Yes it is." My cousin Ocean said coming into the kitchen.

"If you're afraid to leave me O'Rion it's fine. I'll be okay. I don't go for "walks" but you should."

"You sure?"

"Yes!" They all yelled at me.

"Okay, I'll be back."

"I'll be here." She smiled.

Sitting at the table with the women of O'rions family was scary at first but the more I sat and listened to them talk the better I felt. I didn't have a good track record with the females in my life so I was a little apprehensive. They welcomed me with open arms and I was just some strange girl he met at the cleaners. Since my family was so full of shit I often wondered how other people's families were. They were nothing like mine that's for sure. While O'Rion went to go smoke I sat and listened to his mom and Aunt go back and forth over the sweet potatoes recipe.

"I use honey, brown sugar and regular sugar in mine." I found myself saying. "It gives it a different taste."

"You cook Sparkle?" His mom asked.

"Yes. I love it. I don't know how much about me O'Rion has told you but I cook multiple meals a day for my family. I guess over the years I've had time to perfect my craft."

"Well shit give me your recipe then since my mom won't give me hers."

"And I ain't giving you shit. You better hope I write it down before I die."

"Anyway." His aunt replied rolling her eyes. "Tell us about yourself."

"It's not much to tell." I shrugged." I'm twenty, I'm an only child umm I love to bake, cook and sing. That's pretty much it."

"It gotta be more to you than that." O'rions mom said.

"I'm hoping to figure all of that out. O'Rion has been helping me come out of my shell."

"Are you two like a thing?" Sasha asked.

"Oh no." I gasped. "We're just friends."

"You sure cuz I saw the way he looked at you."

"I'm sure. He's just my friend. My only friend to be honest."

"Well do you like him?"

"Sasha leave the girl alone." Her mom Tasha said.

"It's okay Ms. Tasha and of course I like O'Rion. He's nice to me, he helps me. He's done a lot for me in this short period of time more than the people that I live with has done."

"But do you like him like him? When you see him do you feel all warm inside? Do you miss him when he's not around? Do you want to kiss him until your knees give out?"

"Whoa, this is like some of these books I read." I blushed. "Is it hot getting hot in here?"

Fanning myself I was confused when they all started laughing. I knew the oven was on but my body was seriously on fire. Taking a sip of my Dr. Pepper cooled me down slightly but I still didn't get what was so funny.

"I don't understand."

"That's what happens when you like someone. It's totally normal." O'rions mom said.

"I never liked someone before I wouldn't know."

"Girl where have you been living under a rock?" Sasha asked.

"You could say that." I sighed,

"I'm sorry boo I didn't mean to offend you."

"Oh no, it's fine. It's not that, it's just my home life isn't the greatest and being with you guys makes me feel I don't know safe I guess. But it takes a lot to offend me."

"Aww Sparkle. You are safe here baby." His grandma said.

"Thank you."

"Well look my cuz likes you and you like him might as well see what happens."

"He likes me?" I sputtered." Did he tell you that?"

"Well no but I can tell." She shrugged.

"I doubt it. Someone like O'Rion would never like a girl like me."

"And what does that mean?" His mom said like she was offended.

"It's just I mean look at me. I'm ugly, I wear these nerdy glasses, I have nothing going for myself and if I don't get away from my family I probably never will. Why would he like me? It's nothing special about me I'm just Sparkle. Please don't tell him I said that he'll kill me if he heard that again."

"Now that's where you're wrong." His grandma spoke." you're

beautiful on the inside and outside. And from what O'rion tells us you're funny, smart, and you still try to find the beauty in everything regardless of your situation. Do you know how special that makes you? I know them whores you live with give you a hard time but it's probably because they're jealous of you. Don't worry baby were going to work on that confidence."

"I'm speechless, thank you for your kind words. You don't know how much they mean to me."

"I feel like you need a hug." His mom stated.

All I did was nod my head and all the women gathered around and hugged me. I only knew these people for an hour and yet they already made me feel comfortable enough to open up a little and let my worries go. For once I wasn't worried about what my stepmother and sisters would do or say. I was just enjoying my time and that was thanks to O'Rion and his family. The food was heated up and it was time to eat. Orion and his cousins piled back into the house reeking of weed. He made eye contact with me and came rushing over. He pulled me into his arms and kissed me on the forehead. I heard a low giggle and when I looked over Sasha was smiling at us.

"You cool?" he asked.

"Never better." I smiled.

"Good, I know my people can be a lot just wanted to make sure you were okay."

"We took good care of her Ry relax." His aunt said.

"Yes, they sure did."

"Aight good. So can we eat?"

"Boy calm down." His grandma ordered. "Everyone get in here so we can say grace."

His grandma led the prayer as we all sat there and bowed our heads. Her words touched me and sparked something inside of me I never knew was there. I didn't know why the universe sent these people into my life but I was forever grateful. I hadn't known O'Rion long but ever since I met him I've changed. I've become a little stronger, I've opened up and allowed him close to me. Something I never thought I'd be able to do. I always thought I would be the live-in maid until I grew old. I was far away from being away from them but the courage and strength O'Rion gave me made my home life a lot more bearable. O'Rion made me a nice plate and then we all sat around and talked and laughed. I don't think I ever laughed this much in my life. Everyone was so warm and welcoming, it made me wonder what I did to deserve a family like the one I had. Just as quick as the thought entered my mind I looked over at O'Rion and the thought went away just as quick.

Around nine people had started to head home. Orion and I stayed back and helped his grandmother clean up. As people left she gave them their gifts. When she handed me a small gift bag I cried. Inside was some natural hair products, a minute card for my phone, some headphones, and a small diary with a lock. She didn't realize how much those things meant. I don't even remember the last time I got a gift. I wanted to cry again but I held it together. I didn't want them to think I was emotionally unstable. O'Rion grabbed my bag of food and my gift and put it in his car while I said goodbye.

"Thank you so much for allowing me into your home to spend Christmas with you and your family."

"Thank you for coming and allowing us into your life. My grandson is different now. He's happier, he smiles more, he laughs more and it's because of you. He wasn't happy in his last relationship but I hope whatever goes on between you two that the both of you remain happy."

"I hope so too."

"The car is nice and warm for you Spark," Orion said entering the house.

"Okay, I'm ready. It was nice to meet you all and thank you again,"

We took turns hugging his mom and grandma before leaving. We drove in silence the short distance to my house. When he pulled up I started to get out but he stopped me.

"So did you have fun?"

"Fun? Fun is an understatement. Thank you so much Ry. For everything you've done for me."

"Now you calling me ry?" He laughed.

"Everyone in your family calls you that I guess it stuck. Sorry."

"What I tell you about saying sorry? Plus I like how you say it and I'm glad you're finally getting more comfortable around me. So you could call me Ry or Ry Ry I don't give a fuck long as your smiling and happy."

"I'm always happy when I'm around you." I blushed." Can I ask you something though?"

"Anything."

"Was your last relationship that bad?"

"What made you ask that?"

"Your grandma before I left. She said you were happier and smiling more and she believes it's because of me. And they seem to think you like me but I don't see how?" I shrugged.

"We still got a lot of work to do on that confidence of yours but no my relationship wasn't always bad but towards the end, I wasn't myself and now I kinda feel like I'm getting there."

"And why is that? What's changed?"

"You." He simply replied.

I didn't know how to respond. Usually, I was the cause of people's misery. Not their happiness so to hear that from Ry shocked me. I stared at him not knowing what to say back. My mind was racing and my heart was pounding. Orion stared back at me with his big brown eyes glistening under the moonlight. Both of us seemed to be at a loss for words. Orion gently tugged on one of my curls that hung. His handsome face inched slowly closer to mine. His eyes closed and then it happened. My first kiss. His soft lips slowly brushed against mine until they were pressed together, he grabbed the sides of my face and kissed me deeply. I was taken back at first but my body melted after a moment. The kiss didn't last long but it was enough to light my mind body and soul on fire. Orion slowly let go and I opened my eyes. I sat there with my mouth hanging for a moment not sure what to do next.

"I'm sorry."He blurted out.

"Don't be. I-I enjoyed it." I stuttered.

"Let's get you inside."

Orion hopped out of the car before I could say anything. He opened the door for me then grabbed the stuff out of the back seat. We quietly walked to the door the kiss obviously heavy on both of our minds. Unlocking the door I took my coat of immediate and then grabbed the stuff from Orion.

"Thank you again for tonight," I mumbled.

"You're welcome Sparkle. Goodnight."

Orion kissed me on the forehead and then walked out the door. I waited for him to pull off before locking up. Sitting on the couch I let out the breath I had been holding. Tonight was magical and I couldn't have asked for anything better. I only wanted one thing for Christmas besides my mother and that was peace. Tonight I got that and then some. I even had my first kiss.

"Wow! I can't believe it." I breathed.

Touching my lips I felt like it was a dream. But it wasn't, I could still feel his lips pressed against mine. Now I knew what the girls in my books were talking about. If I was standing I probably would have fainted. Getting up off the couch I began putting my food away. Now I had to hide all of my stuff. If Angela found this she would surely kill me. Then my secret double life would be over and I would never see Orion again. I would make sure that would never happen. That was the only peace in my life and I wouldn't let them ruin it. Sitting in my bed I picked up my mom's picture and hugged it tight. Tonight was the best night of my life and hopefully there would be many more to come.

O'RION

Tyree, Jolie and I sat in Dallas BBQ enjoying Henny Coladas and Hennessy wings. We were having a good ass time and I was truly enjoying myself. The last few days I had been in a slump that I just couldn't shake. I found myself just wanting to be left alone. Unfortunately, that meant Sparkle too. I would have still been by myself if Jolie hadn't made me come out with them. Low key I was glad I did I needed to get out of my slump and get a good meal with some good people.

"So what's up with you cuz? You been acting weird the past few days." Tyree asked.

"I know bro, I just ain't been feeling right."

"Anything happen?"

"Man." I sighed. "Where do I begin?"

"From the beginning." Jolie urged.

"You so nosey." I laughed.

"Yup now talk." She smiled.

"So yal remember the girl I was telling you about?"

"Umm sparkle right?"

"Yea well you know the whole backstory with that."

"Yea that shit sad," Jolie replied.

"Facts. But it gets worse. Every year her family leaves her for Christmas to spend time with their family. I didn't want her to be alone so I invited her to come spend Christmas with me at grandmas."

"Aww that's so sweet." Jolie gushed.

"Girl hush and let him finish the damn story."

"Whatever, go head Ry."

"It was a good time. Everyone loved her and she showed me a different side to her. For the first time since we've met, I felt like she was herself. Even though she's still figuring out who she is it was just a side I was glad to see. I was worried about leaving her alone even for a second. I didn't know how she would react or what they would say but it went really well."

"So what's the problem?" Tyree asked confused.

"I kissed her." I sighed

"And," They said simultaneously.

"And I shouldn't have."

"Why not it's obvious you like the girl, so kissing her is expected."

"I don't like her like that," I said.

"I see. You're in denial." Jolie responded.

"Sparkle has been through a lot and shit I just got out of a long term relationship."

"You're giving us every reason why you don't like her but I call bull shit," Tyree stated.

"Me too. Like you said you had been fell out of love with London, so why not open your heart to someone else?"

"Because she's so fragile and I don't think she would be able to handle it."

"How do you know that? I get it she's not used to the real world but from what you've told us it seems like you're prepping her for it. You've been helping her this long you don't think she's taking it all in and trying to learn and grow."

"I do see a difference in her already but she's not there yet and I don't want to push her. But you're right I do like her and I'm struggling with it because I don't know if she feels the same."

"Why don't you just ask her how she feels?" Jolie responded.

"Maybe I will. We talk about everything as is. Guess I'm just scared." I shrugged.

"Let me ask you this. What do you like about her?"

"Everything. From her smile to her personality. The way she makes me feel when I'm around her is surreal. She's unlike anybody I've ever met. She's shy but at the same time very outgoing and she's feisty as hell when she wants to be. Sometimes I can't believe it's the same super shy girl I met at the cleaners."

"Maybe she's not as fragile as you think. Maybe and just hear me out. Maybe she just needs to get out of that situation to really thrive and come into herself. I admire what you're doing for her and you deserve someone for you. London wasn't that person but maybe Sparkle is, you won't know unless yal talk."

"You right I just don't wanna scare her ya know?"

"Give her some type of credit, sheesh," Jolie said rolling her eyes.

"Aight chill gangsta." I laughed.

"Oh shit!" Tyree gasped. "Don't look but London just walked in."

"Perfect just what the fuck I needed,"

"She better hope she don't see us. You know I'm on go." Jolie said taking out her earrings.

"I got bail money baby."

"Good cuz I got a few Henny Coladas in me and I'm with whatever."

"Long as she don't come over here you won't need no bail money."

"Welp she's coming so looks like I might."

Just then London walked up. I didn't even look at her I acted like I didn't know she was there. I knew the way to push London's buttons and for the fun of it was going to do it.

"You don't see me standing here O'Rion?" She spat.

"Maybe he does, maybe he doesn't." Jolie started." Either way the fuck you want? And before you let some smart shit come out your mouth just know I'm on go."

"Jolie!" she breathed. "I didn't come here to fight. I want to talk to O." She pouted,

"We don't got shit to talk about London."

"Just give me five minutes, please. I was going to stop by the apartment but since you're here we might as well get it over with. So can we please talk in private?"

"Look whatever you gotta say just say it aight?"

"Fine. I'm pregnant." She gulped.

"Get the fuck outta here," Jolie said.

"I'm serious." She snapped.

"No, you're not. Did you forget I know when you're lying? You're still tryna get over on me after everything I've done for you?"

"Ry, I'm serious."

"Look at you, you dropped at least ten pounds since we broke up and when you're lying you get this squeaky high pitched voice and you can't even look me in the eyes. So tell me what it really is? You need money don't you. The shit you stole from me before wasn't enough? "

"You don't understand, it's been so hard for me these past few weeks. I just need a few hundred dollars."

"Bitch you're a whole fucking bum. Get the fuck outta here with that shit."

"Ry." She pleaded.

"Does your girl know you're here?"

"Leave her out of this. "She gritted.

"Unbelievable."

"Look I need you Ry don't act like that. Remember the good times we had. All the fun we used to have."

"Yea used to is the keyword. I don't know how you knew I was here but-"

"I saw on Jolie's story." She interrupted.

"I'm boutta block this bitch right now. Sorry Ry."

"I don't care what you need and why you need it but you won't be getting it from me so just go and stay the fuck away from me."

"But Ry."

Standing up I pulled out my wallet and through a fifty dollar bill on the table. That should be more than enough to cover my portion of the bill and then some. Putting on my jacket I dapped up Tyree and hugged Jolie before heading for the door. London was quick on my heels. She was talking a mile a minute but I was just trying to get to my car. Sprinting in front of me she blocked the path to my car. Running my hands down my face I let out a deep sigh. Why couldn't she just leave me alone? Just when I thought life was looking London popped up with some bull shit. I couldn't for the life of me understand why she insisted on interrupting my life. We were over, we would never be friends or anything so why keep trying?

"Look O'Rion if you ever gave a fuck about me you would help me out." She stated.

"And if you ever gave a fuck about me you wouldn't be standing there trying to manipulate me. "

"You know I loved you Ry."

"Only thing I know is you're a manipulative bitch who never gave a fuck about me. I know you used me for your own personal advantage and I also know that you're in trouble." I smiled.

"Why would I be in-."

"I fucking knew it." Her girlfriend yelled interrupting her.

"Babe!" London whipped around and screamed.

"Babe my ass. What the fuck are you doing here? And with him? You told me you were running to the mall and I figured you were lying so I followed you."

"It's not like that at all. Please." she pleaded.

"Well to me it looks crazy as fuck. As much shit as you talk about him and now you up smiling in the nigga face."

"Look I'm just tryna go home so if yal would umm I don't know move I can go," I said nonchalantly.

"Nigga I should have my brothers come fuck you up!" She spat.

"Whatever fuckery yal got going on leave me out of it aight. And fuck you and your brothers. London next time you need money go donate blood or some shit and stay the fuck away from me."

"You here asking this nigga for money. I can't believe you." She screamed.

Once London moved to go calm her down I got in my car and started it up. As I pulled out of the lot I could hear them still screaming at each other. Both those bitches were crazy and they deserved each other. I'm glad I didn't marry her ass, it would have been the biggest mistake of my life. Sometimes I couldn't believe the shit that happened to me. It was still early and I didn't want to go home so I drove around listening to music and enjoying the scenery. My mind kept going to sparkle and I wondered how she was. I hadn't spoken to her since I kissed her and after speaking to Jolie I felt bad. Sparkle didn't deserve that at all. She was too sweet for me to be treating her like shit. Dialing up her number I called her, maybe I would be able to see her.

Sparkle

All night I tossed and turned, I hadn't been sleeping well since O'Rion kissed me. You would think I would be still floating on clouds instead I was confused. He kissed me I didn't kiss him, so I couldn't understand why he was ignoring me. I was confused and hurt. I didn't understand why he was acting like that. After days of waiting by the phone, he never returned my messages. I felt stupid thinking his family was right when they said he liked me. I can't believe a part of me truly believed it. I was so embarrassed I didn't even answer his messages last night when he finally did reach out. Pulling the phone from underneath my mattress I unlocked the phone to see I had 2 missed calls from O'Rion and about five text messages. I quickly looked at them but put the phone away when I heard the front door open. It was quiet for a second then screaming which prompted me to get out of bed to see what was going on. As I hit the bottom of the stairs I heard someone say she's still sleeping. I didn't know what was going on but nobody was dying and the house wasn't on fire. I had the right mind to go back upstairs and get in my bed but I didn't. Walking into the kitchen my mouth dropped.

"Daddy? What are you doing here?"

"Hey pumpkin." He smiled as he turned to face me.

My father looked different since the last time I saw him a year ago. His grey hair started to come in more and he had lost a lot of weight. He was always skinny but today he looked way smaller. I stood there with my mouth open not knowing what to say next. All my anger was building up inside of me. What was he doing here? So many things ran through my mind but then I realized this was my chance to get out of here. Was there really a god out there listening to all my prayers?

"You just going to stand there or are you going to give your old man a hug." He smiled.

I somberly walked over to him and embraced him. When I stepped back I locked eyes with Angela. She mouthed 'You better not say shit'. I rolled my eyes and looked around the room. The girls had these looks on their faces that I couldn't quite read. I didn't pay them any mind and turned my attention back to my father.

"I wasn't expecting you for a few more months."

" I know but we got a few days off going into the new year so I said why not come spend it with my favorite girls." He smiled.

On the inside, I rolled my eyes but on the outside I had the biggest fakest smile on my face. Angela and the girls were staring me down trying to intimidate me. I wasn't intimated in the least if anything this would work in my favor. This was my chance to milk my father for all that I could. I just needed to get him away from Angela.

"Sounds good to me. I just hope we can spend some time together. Like the old days." I pouted.

"Of course matter fact lets go out and grab some food now just me and you."

"Yay." I clapped. "I'll go get dressed."

"Okay hurry I had a long flight and I'm starving."

As I rushed out of the kitchen I saw the looks on Angela's face. I knew she was shaking in her boots but she had nothing to worry about. As long as she didn't act stupid neither would. I couldn't wear any of my new clothes so I threw on a pair of jeans and a sweater. As I was getting my purse together the door swung open. Angela stood there looking like a mad woman.

"Yes?"

"Look here little bitch I tried to stop your father from taking you out but he won't budge. So listen and listen closely."

"No." I flatly said.

"No? No? Did you just no me?"

"Yup." I shrugged." You listen. If you don't want me to say anything you better act right. If I wanna "go out with friends" you're going to let me with no problem. If you object to that then that's fine also."

"Bitch what makes you think he's going to believe you all of a sudden now? He's never believed you before." She smirked.

"Well before I didn't have proof now I do," I smirked back.

"What proof?"

"Test me and find out." I shot back.

"I don't know what or who got you smelling yourself but fucking watch it. He won't be here forever." She said getting in my face.

We stared each other up and down before she stormed off slamming the door behind her. My heart pounded in my chest but at the same time, it felt good to stand up to Angela for once.

"I won't be here forever either," I said to myself.

Shaking her negative energy off me I finished what I was doing. Maybe I could get him to take me to the mall too I thought. As I walked downstairs I caught my father giving the twins and Christiana money. They all hugged and kissed him before running out of the house. Feeling me staring he looked up and smiled at me.

"You ready baby girl?" he asked.

"Yup let's roll."

Walking down the stairs I looked for Angela but she wasn't around. Good, I thought. hopefully, she behaved this week. Grabbing my jacket I followed my father to his rental. The drive was awkward, we barely spoke so I had no idea what to say to my own father and that was sad. Pulling into The Jackson Hole diner I got a little excited. We used to come here all the time when I was younger. All the memories came rushing back and I found myself smiling.

"Burgers?" He asked.

"And Fries with a shake," I replied.

My father got out of the car and ran around to open the door for me. Following him inside we were seated immediately. We skimmed through the menu even though we knew what we wanted. After placing our orders we sat there quietly staring out the window.

"Soooo," I said.

"How have you been princess?"

Okay." I shrugged.

"What's wrong? Is it boy trouble?"

"Uhh no. I don't have a boyfriend?"

"Well, why not? You're beautiful and smart. Any boy would be lucky. Or any girl?"

"No. I like boys dad." I laughed.

"Hey, either way I love and support you."

"Thanks. But no it's not boy trouble."

"If you don't tell me I can't help."

It didn't make sense to even mention what was going on at home. He never believed me so why waste my time. Instead, I decided to use this time to my advantage. I needed money and a lot of it. I didn't care to fuck up what scam Angela had going on with my father anymore. They could have each other just let me be free. I didn't have many life skills but I truly believed I could do it. It would be hard but my life was already hard.

"As you know my 21st birthday is coming."

"Of course how can I forget?" he smiled.

"I don't know what I want to do and it's bothering me."

"You don't have any idea Sparkle? What about a night out in the city?"

"I thought about that but it could get expensive and you know I don't work."

"Don't worry about that princess you only turn 21 once and I want you and your friends to have fun."

Pulling out his checkbook he ripped out a check and filled it in. I eagerly sat there waiting to see how much he was going to give me. This went smoother than expected. Whatever the amount was it wouldn't be enough to really set me up but it'll help. Although I was mad at Orion I knew he would help me make the best of what I had. Passing me the check I looked at it and couldn't believe it.

"$2100?" I gasped.

"Yes, a hundred for every year you've been on this earth. "Reaching out he grabbed my hands and held them with his." I know I haven't been the best father and things over the years have been strained and for that, I am truly sorry. you're my only child and I always thought since you didn't have your mom you needed a mother figure to help mold you into a beautiful woman-"

"But I also needed a father." I interrupted.

"I know Sparkle. Sometimes as parents we don't realize the choices we make aren't always for the best. I've been overseas most of your life and I've missed out on so much. But my love for you Sparkle has never changed."

I didn't really know how to feel about what he said. He was my father and I loved him but I didn't know how I could forgive him. He was the only parent I had and he was barely there for me. He knew how hard I took it when my mother went away and when she went away so did he. I've been on my own ever since. Everything I do and know is because of my mother. The only thing Angela taught me was what not to be life.

"I love you Sparkle."

"I love you too dad," I replied.

Just then our food came. We made small talk while we ate and we even laughed a little. Thankfully I had a state ID so I could eventually cash the check. Angela was forced to get me one and at this moment I was grateful. Leaving the diner I fought with myself if I should ask my father about my mother. He always got quiet when I mentioned her but I needed this bad.

"Father, Can I ask you something?"

"Anything?"

"Did you know my mother was out of jail?"

Glancing over at me he sighed but stayed quiet. He didn't say anything for about five minutes. It was making me nervous the way he was gripping the steering wheel. Maybe this wasn't a good idea.

"Yes. Yes I knew Sparkle."

"Were you ever going to tell me?

"If you asked, but no."

"Why not. Don't you think I deserve to have my mother?"

"You have Angela. She's been your mother for the past ten years or so."

"Angela is NOT my mother." I spat.

"Don't do that Sparkle." He warned. "We had a good night don't ruin it."

"Whatever."

"What's your problem? Yes, you have a birth mother but Angela has been more of a mother to you than she has."

"NO, SHE HASN'T," I yelled. "Just forget I ever said anything."

"Sparkle!"

I didn't even answer him. He sighed and pulled into the driveway. Slamming the door I ran into the house and went straight to my room. How could he say these things? Angela was nowhere near a mother or mother figure to me. She hated me and I hated her. The only reason I didn't go into detail with my father is because I didn't want him to take this check from me. Pacing my room I silently cried I was so frustrated it wasn't even funny. Laying on the bed I pulled out my phone and texted Orion

ME: Hey Ry?

O'Rion: Is everything ok? U haven't returned my calls.

ME: not yet but it will be soon I'm sure of it

O'Rion: Can we meet soon? We need to talk

ME: I'll try...my father is here so she can't say no really

O'Rion: okay keep me posted plz

ME: will do

Putting the phone back under my mattress I laid down and stared at the ceiling. I needed to find a way to see O'Rion. I knew I couldn't just ask, it was never that simple. Angela would try to find some excuse for why I couldn't go out. I wanted to see O'Rion so something would have to give.

"Girls can you come down here." My father yelled upstairs.

I heard the girl's footsteps as they rushed down the stairs. They probably thought he was giving out more money. I waited a second then came out. They were all waiting for me in the kitchen. Standing by the entrance I waited for them to speak. I was still pissed with my father and I didn't really want to be around him.

"Do you guys have any plans for the night?" My father asked.

"Nope." We all replied in unison

"Good, we were thinking of having a movie night. We barely get to spend time together so I thought that would be fun."

"Cool." Christiana replied." We need snacks and lots of it."

"Yes and oo maybe Sparkle can make us cupcakes, She makes the best cupcakes." Ava beamed.

"sure." I shrugged.

"Perfect. "Angela clapped. "And I'll pick the movie."

"Make a list and I'll run and get the snacks." My father offered. "Also any plans for new years?"

"IM spending the night with my boo," Christiana replied.

"And Ava and I are going out too."

"What about you Sparkle?" My father asked.

"Nope don't have any plans," I stated. Angela shot me a look but it was true.

"Aww princess well I wanted to spend some alone time with ANg but that won't change anything. The three of us can do something."

"NO thanks ill just stay in my room. Long as I have snacks I'll leave you be."

"Aww, baby girl you don't wanna spend time with your old man?"

"I'm sure she does babe she just wants to give us some alone time," Angela spoke eyeing me.

"Exactly." I agreed. "Or I can find plans. Doesn't matter to me." I replied eyeing her back.

"On second thought maybe you should stay home. I'm sure you can whip up a nice meal for us."

"MMM I would love that, I miss your cooking baby girl."

"Okay, dad whatever you want."

"Then it's settled I'll go get the snacks and then we'll watch a movie. Before I go can we have a moment alone with Sparkle?"

"Sure." Christiana said." We'll go write our lists."

My father motioned for me to sit down. Nervously I walked to the kitchen table and sat across from them. Angela had this wicked smile on her face and I just knew some bull shit was about to happen.

"So Angela and I talked about our little conversation from earlier. About your mom."

"Wow. I shook my head. I brought that up to you in hopes it would stay between us. I thought I could trust you."

"You can trust me. This is just something we thought we should talk to you together about."

"Why? So yal can keep tryna brainwash me into hating my mother."

"Sparkle." He began.

"No! I don't want to hear it." I snapped. "Ever since you married her yal have been trying to get me to hate her and I never will."

"Sparkle we don't want you to hate her. She's your mom, we just wanted you to be aware that she wasn't a very good person." Angela spoke.

"How would you know? Did you know her or something?"

"I knew her yes." She admitted.

"Wow."

"Look Sparkle I'm sorry I was only trying to protect you not hurt you."

"Well, you did. I don't wanna talk anymore and you don't gotta bring me anything from the store. You guys have fun with your movie."

My father yelled out to me but I didn't care. I wished I never said anything to him. Him running back and telling Angela just proved he was whipped. He was a grown man with no backbone. Granted I didn't have one either but only because they bullied me all these years and he left me alone with them. I still had time to grow and get stronger he was a lost cause. Throwing myself on my bed I screamed into my pillow. I would have texted Orion but I just needed some alone time right now. My father always leaned more towards Angela's kids anyway. I remembered as a kid when he would come home they would get most of his time and when I asked why he said because they didn't have a dad. Well, I didn't either but I guess he didn't see that. Turning on my radio I turned it to the R&B station. Music always calmed me down. Before I could get comfortable in my bed Angela swung my door open. She stood there like a madwoman huffing and puffing once again. The girls came out of there room and stood behind her waiting to see what she would do.

"Sparkle I swear you have got to be the dumbest bitch I ever met. Why don't you listen? HuH? For years you've been asking about your stupid ass mom and every time you get your ass beat for it. So why try to be slick now?"

"Didn't I warn you if you fucked with me while he was here I-,"

"You would what? Huh? The fuck your punk ass gonna do?" She spat.

Angela walked over to me and grabbed me by my hair lifting me off the bed. I fought to get out of her grip but she only pulled harder. I knew this would happen and it's all my fault. I should have known I couldn't trust my father enough to keep it between us.

"Let go of me," I yelled.

"Girls you wanna get some hits in?" she asked.

Christiana was the first to step up. So I screamed and kicked her before she could get to me. Grabbing her stomach she stared at me wide-eyed.

"Fucking bitch." She snapped.

"Get off of me," I screamed louder.

"Sparkle!" I heard.

Just then Angela dropped me as my father ran up the stairs. They all backed away as if nothing was going on. Falling to the ground I sat there trying to catch my breath.

"I came back for my wallet and I could hear you screaming from the car. What's going on?"

"Nothing honey, the girls were just play fighting."

"You're lying." I gritted.

"Watch it Sparkle." My father warned." I don't like your tone.

"No-no-no. I'm tired of this shit. I'm tired of feeling this way. I won't stand here and let you do this again Angela."

"I think maybe you're just having a bad day Sparkle," Christiana said.

"Shut the fuck up please." I snapped." You must have a bad day every fucking day."

"Will someone tell me what's going on?" My father yelled. "Sparkle this isn't like you."

"How would you know?" I sighed. "You don't even care about me.

"I'm your father why wouldn't I care about you?"

"Because you never have!" I screamed." Ever since you left I've been living in fucking hell. I cook and clean and wait on them hand and foot. I'm up before everyone and I'm the last one to go to sleep. I have no got damn friends because I don't go anywhere but to the grocery store and to the cleaners. Oh and once a damn month if Angela is feeling nice she'll give me five minutes in the library to get a book. Other than that, I have to sit here and deal with their fucking abuse and since I have no money and know where to go I'm stuck,"

"Sparkle I send you a check every month." My father replied obviously clueless still.

"Well I've never received a damn penny from it. Look at my clothes, do you wanna see what coat I've been wearing all winter? All Angela does is spend it on hotels so she can suck crack of strange men's dicks."

"Honey, are you going to let her speak to me like this?" Angela whined.

"Sparkle."

"No just save it of course you're taking her side. You used to be such a good father but once you married this one and brought me to live here with her and her bastard kids everything changed. Look at my bruises." I screamed pulling up my shirt.

Tears streamed down my face as I poured my heart out to my father. Angela and her kids stood there speechless. I wish I knew how to fight I would knock their teeth so far down their throat. MY father stood there staring at my stomach. I had black and blue bruises all up my side. There were scratches and even bite marks from Christiana. I couldn't even wrap my mind around this shit right now. I always dreamed of the day I was able to tell my father everything and he believed me. In my mind, he would divorce Angela and we would move far away and mend our relationship. I never thought that day would come but now I had hope.

"' She's fucking lying babe. Right girls?" Angela pleaded.

"Yea Mike. I mean we're girls so of course, we all fight some-times but we're not abusing her." Ava said

"NO, you're fucking lying. I'm fucking miserable here and I finally found my voice to stand up for myself."

"Sparkle I've always looked at you as my daughter. How could you say this?" Angela cried.

This bitch really stood here and mustered up fucking tears. She couldn't be serious right now. I stared at her trying to figure out if I should smack her. MY father looked back and forth between us I guess confused on what to do. When he ran to Angela's side I decided right then and there I was done. He ushered Angela out of the room and the girls followed. Grabbing my cell phone from under the bed I dialed Ry's number.

"Hello."

"Ry." I breathed. "Can you come get me?"

"Is everything okay?" he asked frantically.

"No, not really but I'll tell you when I see you."

"Okay, I'll be outside in ten."

"I'm leaving here now I'll meet you at the pharmacy."

"Okay be safe and I'll see you soon."

"Bye."

Grabbing my runaway bag and my purse I ran down the stairs and out the door. I've had this bag packed for so long just in case I found the courage to leave. Nobody would miss me and I'm sure I wouldn't miss them. He made his decision and I made mine. He had his family and I wasn't in that. I knew that a long time ago I just always had hope. I hurried to the pharmacy to meet Orion. I needed to see him, I needed to feel like it would be okay and he always gave me hope. I spotted his car as soon as I got there. When he saw me he got out the car to greet me.

"What's that?" he asked.

"My runaway bag what the fuck does it look like?" I snapped. He stared at me for a second before his lips curled into a smile.

"They must've really pissed you off."

"You have no idea," I sighed.

"Let's get out of here its cold."

Taking my bags Ry put them in the back seat. He opened the door for me and waited until I was settled to get in. Leaning my head back in his comfortable seats I tried to relax. O'Rion kept staring at me but I just couldn't get my words out. The more I sat there the madder I got. I didn't realize I was crying until O'Rion passed me a tissue.

"Is everything okay Sparkle? You can talk to me about anything."

"I'm just all over the place right now." I cried." I'm happy and sad and just so angry all at the same time. I just don't understand I'm your flesh and blood and I'm literally pouring my heart out and showing you proof and the first sign of a tear you go running to this bitches aide."

"I'm confused."

Taking a deep breath I told O'Rion everything from the beginning. He was shocked that my father was so quick to rush to her side. It just hurt to know my father didn't choose me. Pouring my heart out to Ry made me feel better. He actually listened to me and consoled me. Something I wish my father would have done.

"Damn." Was all he could muster.

"I wasn't going to say anything to my father I was just going to play it cool as long as she did. She had to keep going so I put everything on blast. I showed him my bruises and when she started fake crying he rushed to her side. At that point, I decided I was done so I left. I doubt they even noticed I was gone."

"All of that because you asked him about your mom?"

"Yup. She knew my mom this whole time. I don't know what the story is with that but that shit doesn't sit well with me At least he wrote me a check before all of that happened." I shrugged.

"That's great, how much if you don't mind me asking."

"Twenty-one hundred."

"That'll get you what you need."

"No it won't I have nowhere to go and that'll run out in a week probably. I have nothing, literally the few clothes you gave me and some sweaters I made. Plus I left most of my stuff there, everything in this bag I had packed a while ago. Half of that money will be spent on clothes. Then I need food and a roof over my head. Shit, I should have thought this through."

"Fuck that you're not going back there. You found the courage to leave and I'm proud of you. I'm also sorry that things didn't work out the way you hoped. One day your father will see and hopefully it won't be too late to make amends."

"I want nothing to do with him. I'm officially homeless now and I have no idea what to do."

"Sparkle I have an extra bedroom you can just come stay with me."

"I-I couldn't do that. You've been a great help and you're the reason why I had the balls to tell everyone off in the first place. You've given me more than anybody ever has and I appreciate that but I can't be a burden to anyone anymore."

"You're not a burden Sparkle. I enjoy your company and you can't go back there so unless you wanna go to a shelter I say let's go home." He smiled.

"O-okay but only for a month. After that, I'll find somewhere else to live."

"Okay Sparkle." He replied rolling his eyes.

Twenty minutes later we pulled up to an apartment building. I got out of the car and waited for O'Rion to get my bag. I followed him upstairs to his apartment and I couldn't lie I was nervous and scared. I had never been on my own before I always relied on Angela to take care of me and now I had to take care of myself. O'Rion opened the door and let me enter before coming in and closing the door behind him.

"Well this is it." He said." It's not much but its home."

"It's perfect." I smiled." Thank you again."

"No problem. Come let me show you to your room so you can get settled."

I followed him down the hall to where I would be staying temporarily. It was all white with two-night stands on each side of the bed. It had a TV mounted to the wall with a dresser underneath it. Walking deeper into the room I noticed slight feminine touches. Decretive pillows on the bed and fancy lights on the night tables. His ex-probably helped decorate. At least she had good taste.

"I don't have much food but we can go shopping tomorrow. You wanna order out?"

"Yes please."

"How about Chinese?"

"Perfect. Chicken and broccoli for me."

"Aight cool so take a shower and get comfortable ill order the food now."

"Okay."

"There's already towels and stuff in the bathroom, and extra toothbrushes under the sink."

"Thanks again."

"No problem. Come out when you're done." He said closing the door behind him.

SPARKLE HAD BEEN IN THE BATHROOM FOR CLOSE TO AN HOUR now. I was starting to get worried about her. The food had just come so I laid everything out on the table I had in my living room. I figured we could watch a movie and eat. After I set up the food I started walking towards her door but then she emerged from the door. Her hair was wet and the smell of coconut filled my nose. Even wearing a T-shirt with a few holes in it and some sweat leggings she was still undeniably beautiful.

"I was starting to get worried about you." I smiled.

"Oh sorry. It just felt so good I didn't want to get out." She nervously chuckled.

"It's no problem I just didn't want the food to get cold. Come I set everything up for us."

She followed me to the living room and we sat down on the floor Indian style. I had a few DVDs set out for us to watch. All comedies and hood classics, I figured she could use a good laugh. I handed her a plate so she could start eating. As soon as I passed it to her she piled food onto her plate. I laughed and made my plate.

"So what movie do you wanna watch? I have comedies and hood classics something that will take your mind off of things."

"Hmm let me see." She said picking up the DVDs.

She looked through them and decided on Friday. You could never go wrong with Friday. I could watch that movie a hundred times and it'll never get old.

"I've never seen any of those."

"Damn girl." I laughed." Don't worry we can have movie night again by time you're done with me you'll know these movies like the back of your hand."

"Oooo. I'm so excited." She beamed." I barely got to watch tv I would just listen to the radio most nights after my chores were done."

"Well you can watch all the TV you want here," I said standing up

I put the DVD in and sat back down to finish eating. The movie came on and Sparkle was glued to the tv. I kept peeking over at her to make sure she was enjoying herself. When she laughed she snorted and it was the cutest thing. Her nose would scrunch up, then she would push her glasses up on her face and push her hair behind her ear. She did that every few minutes or so.

"Do I have something on my face?" She turned to me and asked.

"Oh no I'm sorry, I didn't mean to stare. I'm just happy to see you enjoying yourself."

"Oh." She shyly smiled.

"Are you enjoying the movie?"

"Yes, I'm enjoying everything. Even though it's not my ideal situation I'm somewhat happy. You know how on your birthday you blow out a candle and make a wish?"

"Yea." I nodded.

"Every year for my birthday I would get a match and light it. Then make my wish and blow it out. I always wished for a way out and this year I got my wish. Right in time for my birthday."

"When is it?"

"Valentine's day."

"That's next month. Do you have any plans?" I asked. When she looked at me like I was dumb I realized that was a stupid question.

"My bad but don't worry we'll do something."

"Oh no, you don't have to. This is enough."

"I won't take no for an answer. We can have a cake and everything."

"Really?" She asked.

"Yes."

"I haven't had a cake for my birthday since I was like ten. Shit, I haven't had a decent birthday since. That was also the last birthday I spent with my mom."

"Tell me about her."

I could see the way the light brightened in her eyes when she mentioned her mom. I don't know what I would do without my mother. Even though we had fallen out for a few months that was still like my best friend. SO, I could only imagine how she felt for all these years.

"She was amazing Ry. She was my best friend and we did everything together. We would cook and sing together. She taught me how to sew and knit. She taught me everything but how to stay strong apparently. I would sit back and think what my mom would say if she saw me like this. She was the reason I kept pushing through and praying for better days."

"I think you're stronger than you realize and soon you'll see."

"Thank you for believing in me. You've only known me for a short amount of time and you've done so much." She said looking around the apartment." I can cook and I clean trust me when I say ill earn my living."

"You don't have to worry about that Sparkle I only want you to worry about being a better you. Okay?"

"Okay." she smiled.

'Tell me more about your childhood?"

"It was good I had two loving parents, I had friends, I was in sports. Almost every weekend we would go out for the day. A museum or the aquarium. Sometimes we would hop on the train and go into the city for the night and go see a play. Then in the blink of an eye, it all changed. I remember being at home playing when we got a call she was in an accident. Then I noticed the handcuffs. She had fallen asleep at the wheel. That's all they told me. I still really don't know everything. I wish I did though."

"I'm sorry Sparkle. I can only imagine."

"It's so crazy because after that day I never saw her again. She was there one minute and gone the next."

"I don't understand though what made your father leave?"

"At first I didn't know either until we were unpacking and I found my mother's diary. My father didn't believe in bipolar disorder or depression. His parents always told him to pray the devil away. So when he found out my mom was on meds and killed someone he just couldn't take it. I don't know. Any time I would ask about her he would get mad and storm out the room. I didn't understand and I still don't. I probably will never get those answers now." She sighed.

"It's not impossible you never know."

"True." She shrugged. "She always told me I was the sparkle in her eyes that's why she named me sparkle. Plus, her name was Starlyn so she wanted us to both have unique S names." She laughed.

"What is your whole name? Our first introduction could have gone a lot better." I laughed.

"Well I'm Sparkle Raine Blue, I'm twenty and I'm an only child and you are?" She giggled.

"I'm O'Rion Bentley Miller and I just turned twenty-five and I'm also an only child."

"Growing up I used to hate being an only child so when my father married Angela I thought finally I would have siblings but you see how that turned out."

"I did too but I had a lot of cousins my age so it wasn't as bad and for a while. Three of my cousins lived with me and my mom so I was always surrounded by them."

"Lucky you. My father's family is all in North Carolina and my mom was an only child also and her parents are dead."

Sparkle and I sat around for hours just talking. We played twenty-one questions so we could get to know each other even better. She even sang for me and she had an amazing voice. SO good it gave me goosebumps. Sparkle was really something special. I knew I would enjoy having her here. If she thought for a second I was letting her leave after a month she was crazy. She was here now and it was time for her to stand on her own two feet. It was her time to thrive.

"You know the New Year is coming and even though I'm a little sad all of this couldn't have come at a better time."

"Why you say that?"

"New year new start. I can finally just be."

"True. What are your goals for this year?"

"Hmm I haven't thought about it but I would say getting my life together. Staying strong, finding myself and just being happy. What about you?"

"Being happy is high on the list. I want to travel more this year so I'll make that a goal of mine too."

"I want to travel too. I always wanted to go to Paris and Greece."

"We'll get there." I smiled.

Sparkle was getting tired, I could see her fighting her sleep. I knew she had a long day so I didn't bother keeping her up much longer. Once I was sure she was comfortable in bed I headed to my room to shower and get ready for bed. Sparkle and I had a few things to do tomorrow. She needed clothes and toiletries and we needed food. I ate out a lot so I only kept the basics but now I needed to make sure the fridge stayed full for Sparkle. She disclosed to me how they made her eat mostly a cup of noodles while they ate steaks and lobsters and shit. As long as she was at my house she would eat just as good as I would. Before getting in bed I checked on sparkle who was knocked out. Quietly closing the door I went back into my room and got in bed, soon as my head hit the pillow I was out.

THE SMELL OF FOOD JOLTED ME OUT OF MY SLEEP. I HAD BEEN alone in here for so long I forgot Sparkle was now staying with me. Making my way into my bathroom I took care of my hygiene before heading towards the kitchen. Music was playing softly in the background and Sparkle was singing along. Whatever she was cooking made my stomach growl in anticipation.

"Good morning." I greeted entering the kitchen.

"Good morning Ry. Hope you don't mind I made breakfast. One cuz I was hungry and two as a thank you." She laughed.

"Sounds and smells good to me. What you make?"

"I made homemade biscuits and gravy."

"Damn that sounds good as fuck. I haven't had that in years."

"Me either but you had the ingredients so I went for it."

"I didn't even know I had all that. Do ya thang sparkle" I laughed,

"It's almost ready. Just give me a few more minutes."

"Take your time, I'm going to make some coffee."

"So what are your plans for today?" She asked.

"I was thinking we could go get you some clothes and shit, maybe do some food shopping. Whatever you need to do we can."

"I need to cash that check first."

"Okay, there's a check cashing up the block we can do that first."

"Yay." She clapped. "Will you help me pick out some stuff you have a really good sense of style and I don't."

"I got you Sparks."

"Oouu now I have a nickname."

"I guess so, do you like it?"

"I love it."

"I'm glad."

"So is there anything special you want for dinner tonight?" she asked.

"Hmmm I don't really care but I do have a sweet tooth."

"I think I can take care of that for you."

"Cupcakes? Cuz them shits was fire before." I laughed.

"If you want. I was thinking like maybe brownies or something this time. "

"I love brownies, especially with walnuts."

"Only way to have them." she smiled.

"We have so much in common Sparkle."

"We do right?"

"Hell yea it's crazy. I never met someone I had so much in common with."

"Same and breakfast is served."

Spinning around Sparkle presented a beautiful plate of food. She made that shit with love I could tell by the little details. I knew it was a simple meal but the way she cut and layered the biscuits with a spoon full of gravy looked great. I poured us a glass of white cranberry juice and we sat down and ate. Neither of us said a word as we devoured the meal. When we were done we sat there not knowing what to say. I hadn't had a meal that good in who knows how long.

"Sparkle, that was fucking amazing."

"Thanks." She giggled. "I thought so too."

"Damn fuck this shopping I wanna go back to sleep."

"Same. I was hungry but I overate." She pouted.

"How bout we go food shopping and then we can come and watch a movie."

"Deal." She replied.

Sparkle and I got dressed then headed out to handle our business. We cashed her check, got her a few clothes, some toiletries and loaded up on food and snacks. Today was long but it was the most fun I had in a long time. I enjoyed seeing this side of Sparkle. It hurt me to see her when she was down and out. She had such a bubbly down to earth personality. It sucked that her family had damaged her in ways that would take years to undo. If it was the last thing I did I would see to it that she was the best version of herself.

"I'll put the stuff up you go relax.'" I told sparkle as we walked through the door.

"It's okay its kind of late. We stayed out all day. I'm going to start dinner."

"Let's talk first, sit."

"Did I do something wrong?" she squeaked.

"No no no nothing like that. You're free now Sparkle you don't have to worry about that anymore. You're not my maid or my property and I don't expect you to cook every day all day. You took care of them basically all your life. Let me take care of you now."

"I don't know how. Last time someone actually cared about me was..well when my parents were together."

"And that's fine, we'll work on that. I know it'll take some time but we'll work on it together. Okay?"

"Okay. can I ask you something now?"

"Anything."

"The other day when you dropped me off why did you kiss me?"

"Because I like you sparkle."

"You do?" She smiled.

"Of course I do."

"I didn't think you did, to be honest. I just thought you were being nice to me."

"I need to apologize to you."

"Why? You didn't do anything."

"I kissed you then ignored you after. I can only imagine how that made you feel."

"I was really sad, to be honest."

"And for that, I'm so sorry. I felt bad and I distanced myself instead of just talking to you."

"Why did you feel bad, I don't understand?"

"You had so much going on and by me kissing you I felt it would distract you from the real goal. Ya know? Plus I felt like u couldn't handle it because you're so fragile and I'm sorry for that too. I underestimated you because of my own fears not because I really felt like that. I don't want you to think I thought you were weak because that's the furthest thing from the truth. Then I didn't know if you liked me back so yea." I shrugged.

"I am fragile and because of you, I'm going to get better. So no need to apologize, you were right. By the way, I like you too O'Ri-on." She blushed.

"You do?" I smiled

"Of course. Not only are you handsome but you're sweet. Not

just to me but to everyone. You're confident, fearless and just overall amazing. Everything that I wish to be one day."

"I don't think you realize how amazing you really are."

"I don't but I believe one day I will."

"You better." I laughed."How about I cook you dinner tonight? And you can do dessert."

"Deal."

I plugged up my phone and blasted music throughout the house. I know she said she listened to the radio but I was going to put her on to some of the music I liked. Opening the fridge I looked around as I decided what to make. Seeing steak I went for the steak with mashed potatoes and string beans. With Sparkles brownies for dessert, I just knew I was going to gain weight with her living here. We worked good in the kitchen together. Sparkle was on one end whipping up her brownie batter and I was on the other seasoning the steak. She would stop what she was doing every once in a while to watch what I was doing and I would do the same. I could never make brownies from scratch. Once Sparkle was done with the batter she put it in the oven and then left to go shower. I still had a way to go so I rapped along to Nas' One love.

My doorbell rang and since I wasn't expecting anyone I didn't answer. Whoever it was would get the hint and leave sooner or later. Chopping up my onions I put them to the side to get my potatoes boiling. The doorbell went off again, whoever it was didn't get the hint and started pounding on my door. I was starting to get annoyed so I just went to open it. snatching the door open I instantly regretted it.

"What are you doing in here? You didn't hear me ringing the bell?" London asked storming into my apartment.

"What are you doing here London?" I sighed.

"I need a favor." She said matter factly.

"Didn't I tell you the other day to stay away from me? Why won't you listen?"

"Because you're all I have Ry and you promised to always be there for me."

"Yea before you did the fuck shit. Now I just want you to stay the fuck away from me and when I say stay away I mean don't pop up where I'm at. Don't come to my house, don't call me. If it involves me leave me out of it."

"You know what your problem is O'rion?"

"Yea it's you. Look I'm busy." I said pushing her back towards the door.

"You have company?" she asked ignoring my obvious signs that I wanted her gone.

She pushed me out of the way and walked deeper into the apartment. Running my fingers through my hair I sighed. She started walking towards the back room but I grabbed her before she could get any closer.

"That's none of your business. You don't live here and you're not my girl anymore."

"How could you move on this quick? Did you ever love me Ry?"

"Are you fucking kidding me?" I snapped." You fucking cheated on me for a year and left me for a bitch but you're here asking me did I ever love you. I'm really fucking trying here. I promise you I am. I thought one day we could be friends again but I see you just really like taunting me."

"I just didn't expect you to move on so fast. I thought maybe there was a chance you still-"

"Imma stop you right there, there ain't a chance at shit London. You made your choice and I made mine. What we had was good until it wasn't and now that we are no longer together I'm happier than I've been in a while. So in a sense, I thank you for finally allowing me to be happy. Now will you please go."

"I-"

"He asked you to go." Sparkle said entering the living room.

"Her? Really?" London laughed." I thought you liked a more, hmm how should I say this. A high maintenance type of bitch, not a gutter rat."

"I don't even know what a gutter rat is but I won't entertain you. He asked you to go so go." Sparkle snapped.

"First of all bitch this is my old shit you in don't get cute. You out here fucking on my seconds in my shit."

"You don't live here though. I do and I'm asking. No, I'm telling you to leave."

"Ry you need to stop taking mutts of the streets."

"Yea I should have started with you."

London snapped her head my away as if she was appalled that I said that. She looked from me to sparkle before huffing and storming out of the apartment. I was proud of Sparkle. She stood up for me and held her ground when London came for her.

"I'm sorry about that."

"Don't worry about it." she shrugged." I don't like people fucking with you. It makes me upset."

"You heard everything?"

"Basically. I was coming out and I heard a female voice and I got scared at first but then I heard how she talked to you and I didn't like that."

"You looked like you were ready to fight." I laughed.

"I felt like it." she smiled." I can't fight for shit but I won't let no one mess with you."

"Same here."

Picking sparkle up I spun her around. She giggled in my arms and my heart pounded in my chest. At this moment I realized I could see a future with Sparkle. I hadn't known her long at all but she made me feel things that nobody else had ever come close too. I was beginning to believe my grandma when she said relationships brought together by fate were the most powerful. In my heart, this felt right. I don't know about her but I was beginning to fall for her. Kissing her forehead I put her down so I could finish cooking.

"ill help you cook since this meal is nowhere near done." She laughed.

"You can do the mash while I get started on the steaks."

"These brownies look perfect." She said pulling them out of the oven.

"I can't wait to fuck them up with some ice cream."

"Hurry with the steaks so we can dig in."

"Okay, I'm going."

"So I was thinking since I'm staying here now ill go get the rest of my stuff. It's not much but I need my radio and my pictures of me and my mom."

"I can take you before work. I need to go to my grandma's any way to pick up something. "

"that works for me, I only need like ten minutes. They're usually out of the house around eleven. I don't want to run into them at all. Hopefully, I never see any of them again."

"And if you do ill be there to protect you."

"I know." She blushed.

Sparkle and I finished up our meal and sat down to eat. I lit a few candles and put Pandora on an R&B station. The more we got to know each other the better it would get. Sparkle and I laughed and ate until we couldn't eat anymore. I couldn't remember the last time I had this much fun just hanging around the house. Sparkle wanted to watch next Friday so I popped that in while we ate brownies and ice cream.

Sparkle

Every day that I woke up not in that house was a great day for me. For years I had been subjected to their torture and I was finally free. Ever since I left I began having nightmares. I always woke up back in my old room with Angela and the girls hovering over me with knives. I would wake up just before Angela would stab me. O'rion already worried enough about me so I didn't plan on bothering him with my silly nightmares. Standing on the balcony I breathed in the crisp winter air as I sipped my coffee. Ry was getting ready for work and I was just waiting on him. He was going to take me to the house then drop me off here before going to work. I didn't really want to be alone but I had to suck it up. I used to being alone anyway this should be nothing new. Once I got situated I would find a job and start my new life.

"Spark you okay? " O'rion asked coming out onto the balcony.

"Yea why wouldn't I be?"

"I heard a noise coming from your room and when I walked in you were tossing and turning. I went to wake you but then you just got this peaceful look on your face so I let you be."

"Oh," I mumbled.

"Are you having nightmares?"

"Yea I don't usually have nightmares but ever since I left there I've been having them. I didn't want you to worry so I didn't say anything."

"I don't want you to be afraid to tell me things Sparkle."

"It's not that I'm afraid it's just I don't want you thinking I'm not making any progress."

"I would never think that. You've been making progress since the day we reconnected at the party. And I'm very proud of you."

"Thanks." I blushed.

"Next time you have a nightmare my room is always open.

Don't be afraid to come to me about things your feeling or going through. I know this transitioning period is hard for you."

"Thanks, Ry its means a lot."

"It's me and you Sparkle." He smiled.

"ME and you."

"You ready to ride?"

"Yup. I really shouldn't be long so by the time you go handle your business I'll be outside waiting. I don't wanna stay in there longer than I have too."

"I got you."

The drive to the house had my stomach doing backflips. I don't know why I was so nervous but I was. I just couldn't shake this uneasy feeling. Then again I did blow up their spot and ran away. When we pulled up in front of the house Angela's car was gone. I just hoped the girls were gone too.

"If I'm not here when you come out just call me we can stay on the phone until I get back."

"Okay. Will you stay here until I see if the house is empty?"

"Of course."

Grabbing the bag Ry let me borrow I got out the car and walked up the stairs. I checked my surroundings before going in. This would probably be the last time I would step foot in this house. I should be rejoicing I was free but a part of me wasn't jumping for joy. It all just seemed too good to be true. Calling O'rion I let him know the house was clear and he was free to go. Running up to my room I quickly through my radio and all my pictures in my bag. I grabbed a few more clothes and then snuck into Angela's room to get my birth certificate and social security card. She kept everything in an unlocked box under her bed. I got down on my knees and pulled the box out. She never let anybody look in here I had no idea what else she could be keeping. Opening the box I found what I was looking for immediately. I rummaged through the box just being nosey. I found a group of pictures and started looking through them. There were baby pictures of me and even school pictures. I took all the pictures of me it's not like she needed them. As I looked through the box I found a picture of my mom and Angela.

I knew they knew each other but by looking at the picture it looked like they were really close. What could have happened between them? Hearing the door slam I hurried and put everything back and got out of Angela's room. Tiptoeing back to my room I through everything in there and stood still. Hopefully, they would be in and out. When I heard footsteps coming up the stairs my stomach dropped to my toes.

"What is this door doing open?" Angela said entering the room." Oh, look who decided to come back home."

"I'm not staying I just came to get some stuff."

"That's funny last time I checked you had no friends and nowhere to go. "

"I'd rather live in a dumpster than stay here."

"Do you want to know why I hate you so much?" She blurted out.

"I would love too."

"When I was sixteen your mom and I met your father. I saw him first and I thought he was just the sexiest guy but your whore as mom got to him first. They began dating and I was furious. She was my best friend and she should have known I liked him after we met him. She went for him anyway. I always thought he would see that I was the one for him. I wasn't fast, I was smart and funny. All the qualities he needed. We would all hang out and do stuff together. Over time I got tired of playing the third wheel so I stopped coming around so often. I just wanted to see if he would start asking about my whereabouts but he never did. They got married and he put her up In this big house. While I was on my second pregnancy by a fucking bum. When your mom told me she was pregnant I was devastated. I always thought there was a chance we could still be together.

"What does that have to do with your hatred for me?"

"DON'T YOU SEE!." She yelled." Your mom didn't deserve him. After sleeping around with everyone she wasn't supposed to get the good life. I was but instead, I was pregnant by another no good nigga and she was living life. Traveling the world, he put her through college and everything. I always thought yea they're married but all I need is one shot and he would be mine. Then you came and he was smitten with you and I knew I lost him for good."

"So you hate me because my mom took the guy you wanted? Did it ever cross your mind that he didn't want you? Did you ever stop to say hmm maybe I'm bat shit crazy and need to reevaluate my life?"

"YOU AND YOUR MOM HAD THE LIFE I WAS SUPPOSED TO LIVE." She screamed. "I should have been the one with his children and you should have been swallowed or aborted I don't give a fuck."

"You're a sick bitch and I'm glad I don't have to be here anymore. You and your children need serious help and I hope you get it. At least you finally got your wish now you and him can live happily without me in the picture."

"Mom!" Christiana yelled upstairs.

"What?" she snapped.

"What's taking you so long? We're hungry?"

"Tell your sisters to come inside our maid is back she'll cook for us."

"No, the fuck I won't."

Grabbing my duffle bag I ran out the door. By time I got downstairs, the girls had come in. They swarmed around me not letting me get out the door. Looking behind me I saw Angela was blocking my path to get out the back door.

"Good to see you're back," Christiana smirked.

"Won't be for long," I replied trying to not show how afraid I was.

"And why not? You have a lot of making up to do. You have a few meals to make up for. There's laundry and cleaning that needs to be done. And since you told your father we had to do a lot of lying and ass-kissing to get him to fall back."

"That's not my problem. Speaking of my father where is he?"

"He went to get a haircut. In the meantime, you need to figure out how you're going to make this up to us. I swear to god if this doesn't get resolved before he leaves your life will be even more miserable." Angela answered.

"That's between yal. I'm leaving and I'm never coming back. So good luck finding someone else to ruin. Oh, wait you still have my father." I shrugged.

"Oh please." Angela waved me off." Where can you possibly go? You have no friends and you have no money."

"That's information for me to know and for you to never find out. Have a nice life."

Clutching my bag I began walking towards the door. Someone grabbed me by the hood of my coat and through me to the ground. The bag broke my fall but the force from being pulled hurt my throat. Angela and the girls surrounded me staring me down. I was terrified and I tried not to show it but I knew they knew I was scared.

"If you think you're going to leave this house that easy you got another thing coming," Angela said.

"What are you going to do me?" I trembled.

"Don't worry about that. Just know I'm tired of your shit Sparkle now it's time to pay for your mistakes."

"The only mistake I made was coming back here. You bitches will never amount to anything. You thought you could break me and even in my weakest times, I was still stronger than you. Look at yourselves. DO you see how pitiful you are? Four of you big ass bitches against little ol' me. How are you going to explain this to my father huh?"

"Simple." Christiana shrugged. "You're going to tell him someone attacked you when you ran away. You were sleeping in the streets some guy or girl whatever you chose I don't give a fuck beat you up."

"Yea like that's going to work."

"It will don't forget he'll only be here a few more days. So if he doesn't that's on you."

"I hate you." I spat.

"Likewise," Ava replied.

"Twins hold her down," Angela ordered.

They charged at me grabbing me by my arms and legs, I kicked and screamed with everything in me but they were literally each twice my size. Ava was above me holding my arms flat against the floor. I struggled underneath their grip but it wasn't much I could do. Angela paced in front of me before stopping to talk to Christiana. They were whispering to each other so I couldn't hear. Ava was so into their conversation she didn't realize she was loosening her grip. Soon as she did I shot up, using my forehead I clipped her chin.

"Fuck! My tongue." She screamed out.

"That's what you get." I spat.

Angela ran up on me and punched me in the face. My head snapped back and my glasses flew off for a second I forgot where I was. One by one I felt all of there fists and feet on me. I tried to cover my body from the blows but it was no use. Four sets of hands and feet were everywhere. I allowed my mind to take me to my happy place until it was all over. That's what I usually did to get through there beatings. It was never this bad before and with each hit, I felt myself losing consciousness. Blood poured from my nose and my lips were busted. My vision blurred and all I could think about was O'rion. I knew he would be wondering where I was. I hope he would never stop fighting until I was free. Who was I kidding? Was I even that important for him to go that hard for me? I doubt it. As I laid there my thoughts went to the day I met Ry. Back then I didn't know it but it would become the best day of my life. It was the day my life changed. They kept hitting me over and over again. With every hit they cursed my name, called me everything but a child of God and all I could do was curse my father for putting me in this situation.

"Fuck Mike Is calling we gotta go pick him up," Angela announced. "Sparkle get yourself together before we get back."

I felt three kicks to the stomach and then someone whispered in my ear that they were sorry. It had to be Asia. I couldn't muster up the energy to respond. I wanted to tell them to kiss my ass instead I just laid there trying to breathe. Tears stung my eyes as I wept. Why did I come back here? Hearing my phone vibrate gave me a burst of energy. If I could get to my bag I could get help. Crawling the few feet to my bag seemed impossible. My ribs hurt and I couldn't breathe. The room spun around me but I kept pushing until I got there. Unzipping the bag I searched for the phone. With no glasses and swollen eyes, I could barely see. The phone stopped ringing soon as I pulled it out. Unlocking it I called Ry back.

"Sparkle are you ok? I been calling you?"

"Ry! Help me."

Leaving my grandma's house I called Sparkle to let her know I was on my way. When she didn't answer the first two calls I started getting nervous. I knew this was a bad idea. I should have followed my gut and stayed with her. If anything happened to her I would never forgive myself. My grandma only lived a few blocks away but I still couldn't get there fast enough. My phone rung snapping me out of my trance. Sparkle's name popped up on my dashboard and I finally could breathe.

"Sparkle are you ok? I been calling you?"

"Ry help me." She answered. Then the phone went dead.

"FUCK!" gripping the steering wheel I pushed heavily on the gas.

Speeding through the back blocks I ran through all the stop signs. I didn't stop until I got to Sparkle. Parking sloppily in the driveway I left the car running. Two steps at a time I ran up the porch steps. Peeking through the door I could see a silhouette on the floor. My stomach dropped when I opened the unlocked door. Sparkle was laying there not moving. Trickles of blood were splattered all over the floor. Running over to her limp body I scooped her up in my arms. Looking down at her face my heart broke. Her lip was busted, her eyes were swollen and her nose was broken I could tell from looking at it.

"Sparkle wake up." Gently shaking she winced as she slowly opened her eyes.

"Ry." She groaned.

"What the hell happened?"

"Evil bitches." She whispered as she fell back out.

"Shit. I'm gonna get you to the hospital Spark. Hold on."

After grabbing her bag I scooped Sparkle into my arms and rushed to the car. Gently placing her in the front seat I rushed to the driver's side and sped off. How could these people do this to her? And how could her father allow this to happen? I didn't understand it at all. If I had my way Sparkle would never see these people again. I knew it wouldn't take much convincing but still, these people didn't deserve to have someone as special as Sparkle in their lives. I made it to the hospital in no time. Parking the car I grabbed Sparkle and brought her inside the emergency room. Seeing her limp body the nurses grabbed her immediately but they stopped me at the door. I pleaded with them to let me go with her but they said I had to wait. Feeling defeated I sat in one of the chairs and waited for them to come and get me.

OVER AN HOUR HAD GONE BY AND I WAS FINALLY ABLE TO SEE Sparkle. They had her set up in her private room. When I walked in she was sleeping. Pulling up a chair next to her bed I sat down and reached for her hands. Rubbing them softly I stared at Sparkle. Her ribs were fractured on top of everything else. Even with a swollen face, she was still the most beautiful girl in the world. she was still perfect. Her eyes fluttered as she looked around the room taking in her temporary home for the next few days. When our eyes met she smiled at me but all I could do was shed a tear.

"Am I dying or something?" she breathed.

"No."

"So why the long face Ry?"

"I should have been there. I shouldn't have left you by yourself."

"It's not your fault. It's mine, I wanted my stuff so bad I shouldn't have gone back there. What's done is done."

"You can press charges against all of them. When you get better we'll go handle that."

"Nah, I'm good."

"You're not going to make them pay for what they did to you?"

"They're going to pay but I'm not going to waste my energy on them. A new year is about to begin I just want to focus on me. Karma will handle them, I have so much more to look forward to."

"I admire your optimism Sparkle. I really do. I wish I was more like you."

"ill rub some of my optimism onto you." She smiled.

"Please do."

"Thank you for everything you've done for me. Thank you for being there for me. Thank you for caring about me."

"You don't have to thank me Sparkle. I would do it again if I had to. I wouldn't change anything besides you ending up here."

"Me either. The day I met you changed my life and I didn't realize it until today. I never would have thought one encounter at the cleaners something I do all the time would change me, change my life. I never thought I would be free and all though I'm laying in a hospital bed with a fractured rib I feel on top of the world. I will never forget the day we met. It's the most important day of my life."

"I'll never forget the day I met you either. my life changed in ways I never would have imagined. You bring happiness to my life. You bring something to my life that I never knew I needed until I met you. And as long as I'm around ill there to protect you."

"I know." She yawned.

"Get your rest Spark, ill be here when you wake up."

Sparkle drifted off to sleep and I sat there and watched her for a while. The doctor had told me it would be a six-week recovery so I shifted my work schedule to accommodate Sparkle and whatever she would need. At this point, I couldn't see my life without her. The world has a way of putting people together who otherwise would probably never cross paths. The day I met Sparkle I was supposed to pick up my suit thirty minutes earlier but I was procrastinating. If I would have gone when I was supposed to I would have never met her. I wouldn't have gotten to spend those twenty minutes with her that was etched into my mind. If I didn't go to that party she would have remained the beauty who's name I never got. Our relationship was brought together by fate in more than one way and I realized that now. I wouldn't want it any other way.

The recovery process has been slow and agonizing but here I was with the all-clear to resume normal activities. The past six weeks I couldn't do anything and even when I tried O'rion didn't let me. He took care of my every need and I didn't want for nothing. Between him, his grandma and his cousin's wife Jolie I was well-taken care of. I couldn't have asked for a better support system in my time of need. I don't know how I would repay them but I would if it was the last thing I did. I sat in the waiting room of my doctor's office waiting for Ry. He had to work early so Jolie dropped me off and he was picking me up. I couldn't wait to give him the good news. I could imagine how tired he was of the boring routine we had become accustomed to. We woke up, ate breakfast together and then he would go to work. When he got off we would order take out and then watch movies until we fell asleep. Over the six weeks, we had grown so much closer. It was like I finally had a family. My phone vibrated In my hand, when I looked down it was a text from Ry.

Ry: I'm pulling up now

Walking outside Orion was already parked out front waiting for me. When he saw me he got out to greet me. Kissing me on my forehead he opened the door and waited until I was situated before getting back into the driver's side.

"So any good news?" he asked pulling into traffic.

"Yes! My doctor said I'm all healed."

"that's great Spark. I know how anxious you were."

"And now I can finally get my life started."

"Exactly. So what do you want to do first?"

"Cook."

"Really?" he laughed.

"Yes, I need a good home-cooked meal."

"So what you're tryna tell me is you don't like my cooking?"

"I love your cooking Ry but I've missed cooking so that's first on my to-do list. I have all the ingredients already so that's what I'm gonna do."

"Okay I gotta drop you off, I gotta few errands to run and then ill be back."

"Okay, what time so I can make sure dinner is ready."

"Hmm around eight."

"Perfect now I can get a nap in."

"You and your naps." He smiled.

Ry dropped me off at home and went to go handle his business. I tried taking a nap but I was just too excited. So I turned on my speaker and blasted music while I cleaned. I finally had the freedom to move how I wanted to since I no longer had a fractured rib. I danced and sung my heart out until I got tired. Ry would be home soon so I got started on dinner. I made homemade biscuits, fried pork chops, mashed potatoes and string beans. Soon as the biscuits came out the oven the front door opened.

"Mmmm something smells good." He said entering the kitchen.

"Thanks and you're just in time. As always." I laughed.

"My stomach just knows when its time to come home. I see you couldn't wait to do some cleaning."

"you know it. I hated being confined to the couch. Now that I can move freely you better be ready."

"Ready for what?" he asked sitting at the kitchen table.

"To be on the move, it's so many things I want to do now that I'm better."

"We can do whatever your heart desires." He smiled.

"Yay."

After fixing our plates we sat in the living room and watched a movie. He had put me on to all the hood classics and after being on bed rest I've watched some of them multiple times. I really enjoyed these moments of peace. Orion brought so much peace to my life which was something I never thought I would have. Since I cut my family off for good things had been looking up for me. Those bitches could have my father. I didn't need any of them all I needed was those who cared for me. It was almost midnight when Orion said he had to run out. That was weird but I didn't say anything. Instead, I just cleaned up our mess and waited for him to get back.

———

RUSHING TO MY CAR I GRABBED THE GIFTS I HAD BROUGHT for Sparkle. Tomorrow was her 21st birthday and I'm pretty sure she forgot. I didn't though and it was going to be a special birthday if it was the last thing I did. With everything going on she needed this. She deserved this. She had healed so much mentally and physically I was so proud of her. I stood outside the door to our apartment at 11:59. At twelve on the dot, I wanted to be the first to wish her a happy birthday. When the clock hit twelve I entered the house but she wasn't in the living room.

"Spark where are you?"

"In the kitchen." She replied.

Quickly lighting the candle on top of the cupcake I entered the kitchen.

"Happy birthday Sparkle," I yelled.

"Oh my god! "She cried. "Thank you, Ry."

"Make a wish."

She closed her eyes and made her wish before blowing out the candle. I gave her the cupcake but she insisted on sharing it with me. I pulled out a carton of ice cream and scooped us some into a bowl. She cut the giant cupcake in half and we dug in.

"I totally forgot my birthday."

"I figured. Its been a lot going on but I promise it'll be the best birthday ever."

"It already is." She smiled at me.

"What do you want for your birthday?"

"I have everything I could ever ask for honestly."

"You sure?"

"I mean I would love to find my mom but I've been scared to start looking again. Don't want to be disappointed."

"Don't worry Sparkle, ill help you. We'll find her together."

"Really?" she gasped jumping into my arms.

With her arms wrapped around my neck, she hugged me tightly. She smelled heavenly, like coconuts. It made little me excited but I shifted my mind to other thoughts. She must've sensed my hesitation because she jumped back into her seat.

"Sorry." She mumbled.

"Don't be I enjoy having you in my arms," I admitted.

She blushed which made me blush but it was true. Sparkle lit a fire deep inside of me and nothing could put that fire out. She did something to me, she made me feel again. When the time was right I would make things official but for now, I just enjoyed her. Even though we had already admitted our feelings for each other we both still were taking things very slow.

"Are you tired? I know today was long?"

"A little but I want to watch The Chappelle show."

"Okay, ill set it up you go put on your Pajamas."

Watching Sparkle skip out of the room I smiled. Her bubbly personality could make the meanest and grumpiest person smile. After getting the Tv set up to watch her new favorite show I grabbed a blanket out of the hallway closet. I grabbed us some drinks and snacks. She came back and we cuddled on the couch as we watched The Chappelle show. After a half-hour, I didn't hear her laugh I looked at her to find her sleeping. I called out her name but she didn't budge. Turning the TV off I cleaned up our mess before picking her up and carrying her to the bed. I tucked her in and kissed her on her forehead before leaving.

THE SUN WAS SHINING AND THE BIRDS WERE CHIRPING. Well, not really but I felt like I could hear birds chirping. I had just got out of the shower and was ready to get my day started. I hoped O'Rion was awake. I was so happy I couldn't sleep. I woke up feeling on top of the world. Today was my birthday. Since I usually didn't celebrate it became just another day. Now I actually had something to celebrate and someone to celebrate with. Walking out of my room I smelled food and heard soft music playing. I walked into the kitchen and it was filled with red and pink heart-shaped balloons. Happy birthday banners were hanging on the wall and on the table, there was a big twenty-one sign. O'rion was standing over the stove in nothing but his basketball shorts. Seeing his almost naked body made me hot and flustered. I wanted to turn around and go back to my room but I couldn't. I had never been so hot and bothered before but Ry was just so sexy. From his dimples and muscular arms to his eyes and his smile. Most importantly his heart turned me on the most. I didn't know where we really stood in our relationship but sex was something I was looking forward too. I wasn't quite ready but when the day came I knew it would be magical. There was nobody else I would rather give myself to than him.

"Hey birthday girl. Good morning." O'rion smiled.

"Good morning." I smiled.

"Sit down I made you a nice birthday breakfast."

"Wow thanks. You didn't have to."

"Chill Sparkle. It's your birthday."

"Fine." I laughed

I sat down and when I did O'rion placed a gold birthday crown on my head. He then placed a birthday sash across my body. I wanted to thank him again but I couldn't find the words. They were caught in my throat. He came back with a plate piled with food. He made French toast with whipped cream on top, bacon, eggs and fresh fruit on the side. Everything smelled so good I couldn't wait to dig in but I was going to wait for O'rion first.

"Orange juice or cranberry?" He asked opening the fridge.

"Cranberry definitely. You know this."

'I know just wanted to ask you might've switched up today." He laughed."I'm glad I met someone who loves cranberry juice and Dr. Pepper as much as I do.

"And I'm glad you're a Harry Potter fan."

He finally sat down so we could eat. Once he started eating I dug in myself. We made small talk as we ate. He told me he had a few things planned for today and I couldn't wait. When we finished eating he told me to go wait in the living room while he washed the dishes. I walked around the living room looking at all the pictures. He had baby pictures of himself and what I assumed were his cousins. He had a lot of football trophies and articles on him from when he played. I read some of the articles and they were amazing. I've read them a few times now when he wasn't here.

"Those were some good times," O'rion replied.

"You were really good," I said to him.

"I was. Sometimes I wonder what my life would be like if I went to the NFL I don't think about it much anymore. Come let's sit I have some gifts for you to open."

"O'rion you didn't!" I gasped.

"Come one Sparkle. You told me you haven't had a good birthday in years and with all you've been through you deserve it so come on." He said pulling me over to the couch.

He made me sit on the couch while he disappeared into his room. He came back with two huge birthday bags. He sat them in front of me and I all I could do Is sit there. He placed the first one in front of me and I ripped the tissue paper out of the bag. I was so excited I couldn't help myself. I pulled the stuff out one by one admiring each item for a second. The first bag was filled with pajamas and bath and body works products. There were a pair of slippers in there and a nice plush robe. He even got me lots of natural hair products. Most brands I had never tried because they were way too expensive.

"Thank you so much."

"no problem. I knew you needed some stuff."

"Some?" I laughed." I need a lot."

"Here open this one. I hope I got the sizes right if not we can take them back."

The second bag had five pairs of jeans in different washes, there were also a pair of black riding boots that were so nice and they were the right size. He also got me a few sweaters, long sleeve t-shirts and cute socks. Then he pulled a box from out of the table. It was a white box with a big red bow on it. Smiling at him I slowly undid the bow and took off the top. I tore open the tissue paper and inside was a black Michael Kors purse. It had a big gold lock in the middle and gold links for the handles. It was perfect. When he pulled out a second box I just about fainted. Inside was a black bubble coat. The fur around the hood was so soft. I finally had a decent winter coat. Looking at all the stuff I had and finally, the tears I had been holding in fell free. O'rion pulled me into his arms and just held me. I was overwhelmed but a good overwhelmed. What did I do to deserve all of this? I was still having trouble believing this was my new life.

"Shh don't cry Sparkle. It's your birthday and it valentine's day."

"If you haven't noticed by now all I do is cry." I laughed. "But they're good tears."

"Good I'm glad now go put on one of these outfits so we can go."

"Wait where are we going?" I said wiping my tears.

"Youll see."

O'rion helped me bring my stuff to the room and then left me to get dressed. I had so many great things I didn't know what to wear. I laid everything out and then decided on a pair of dark blue jeans with the red sweater and the boots he got me. The way the material felt against my skin made me feel like a princess. I know they're just clothes but Angela always said good material will always feel like velvet on your skin and these jeans did. I looked in the mirror he had hanging on the back of the door and admired myself. The jeans fit me perfectly. For once I felt like a woman. My curves were on full display instead of being hidden. Angela always teased me because I had a big butt but she was just mad she had a pancake booty. Walking out of the room I found O'Rion sitting on the couch playing around on his phone. He was dressed similarly to me, he had on a red sweater with dark blue jeans and a pair of black timbs on. I wonder how he knew what I was going to pick. When he heard me enter the room he turned and looked at me. Smiling he got up, walking towards me he grabbed my hands and twirled me around.

"You look great."

"Thank you. I feel great."

"Good, let's go we got a long day ahead of us."

First, we went to the nail salon near his house. He paid for me to get a manicure and Pedicure and even my eyebrows. Since he was paying I let him choose the color. He chose a nice light pink color which I thought looked great with my skin tone. After that, we went to a spa where we got an hour-long massage. They gave us strawberries and champagne to enjoy before we got our massages. Being myself around O'Rion seemed to come naturally. We sat and talked the whole time while we waited. I had never had champagne before and I didn't get all the hype. It was nasty but once O'Rion dropped a strawberry in it the taste seemed to get better. As we talked O'Rion would place his hand on my leg or brush a stray hair out of my face. Whenever he would touch me sparks ignited deep within. I don't know if he noticed but I got a little flustered each time. The massages were so relaxing that we both fell asleep fifteen minutes in. When they were done I felt like a whole new person. This was the best birthday ever. This was more than I ever expected. I was living in my own little fairy tale for once my dreams were coming true.

"O'Rion this was the best day of my life," I said as we walked to the car.

"It's not over yet Sparkle."

"This is the most excitement I've had in a while." I laughed.

"good I like seeing a smile on that beautiful face." He replied opening my door.

"Beautiful?"

"Yes." He smiled." You don't think you're beautiful?"

"I don't know. I was always told I was ugly."

"Well, you're not. You're beautiful not only outside but inside and don't ever let anyone tell you otherwise again." He replied sternly.

"I won't." I blushed.

"Good."

He kissed me on my forehead before closing my door. He got in the driver seat and pulled into traffic. He thought I was beautiful. I had never been told that before. O'rion was the sweetest person id ever met. It was the little things he did throughout the day that made today even more special. From opening doors to helping me put my jacket on. He was everything and I don't know what happened with his ex but she was missing out. We pulled back into his apartment complex and parked. When we hopped straight in an uber I was a little confused but I just went along for the ride. I stared out the window wondering what he had planned next. This day was already more than I imagined. I didn't care if we stayed home and watched Friday again. We made it to Jamaica train station and I waited for him to buy our train tickets. I still didn't ask any questions. As long as I was with O'Rion I knew I was safe. We stood on the train platform waiting for the next train. We still had about ten minutes before the next one came. O'rion pulled me into his arms and wrapped them around my body. I instantly relaxed and was all of a sudden hot. Very hot. I stood there listening to his heartbeat until the train came. When it did we found a two-seater and sat down. He pulled out his phone and plugged in his headphones. He put one in his ear and the other.

Listening to the type of music he liked helped me get to know him better. He seemed to love R&B and old school hip hop. Some of the songs he played reminded me of my childhood. My mom and I would clean on Sundays and listen to music. We would end up doing more singing than cleaning. We arrived at Penn Station and then hopped on the subway. As we walked I saw all the couples out celebrating Valentine's day and for once I wasn't jealous. All though O'Rion wasn't my man he had made this Valentine's Day and birthday spectacular.

"Have you ever been ice skating?" He asked.

"Never but I always wanted to."

"Good." He smiled.

Soon as O'rion and I got to the rink we got our skates and made our way to the ice. I was excited, I just hoped I didn't fall. O'rion got on the ice first and held his hand out. Taking his hand I slowly stepped onto the ice. It was slippery at first and I almost fell bet Ry caught me.

"It takes a little getting used to but it's easy I promise."

"Okay but if I fall you better fall with me."

"You won't fall, I got you." he smiled."

We slowly made our way around. Ry was right after a while I got used to it. I wasn't going to tell him that though. I loved how our hands felt intertwined with mine. it felt like where I was supposed to be. I knew nothing about love and relationships but this felt right. It was like my dreams but better. Slow jams played in the background as all the couples skated around the rink. O'rion and I Skated to the middle of the rink were people were slow dancing. Placing my arms around his neck Ry held onto my hips as we swayed to the beat. I was much shorter than him but I was still able to look into his eyes. Those beautiful eyes that made me melt.

"Are you having fun?"

"Am I? This is the best."

"" Good. I just want to make you happy Sparkle." he smiled.

"I am happy Ry. How could I not be? You make me feel things I've never felt before. You make me feel like I can do anything I put my mind too. This is the happiest I've ever been. I don't know if ill ever feel like this again." I admitted.

"You will, this is just the beginning I promise."

Neither of us said anything after that. We just danced. Resting my head on his chest I listened to the beat of his heart. I didn't hear the music or the people anymore. It was just the two of us, alone holding each other. Ry leaned down and kissed me on my forehead. I loved it when he did that. Smiling up at him my breath got caught in my throat when he bent down to kiss me. It was just a peck at first, making my body shiver from his touch. Closing my eyes I pressed my lips against his. He was shocked at first but continued kissing me slowly. Slipping his tongue into my mouth my knees buckled. The taste of mint danced on my taste buds giving me a high I never knew I needed. O'rion slowly released me, staring deep into my eyes he brushed a curl out of my face, tucking it behind my ear.

"Sorry. I got carried away." He breathed.

"it's okay I've been dreaming of that all night."

"I don't want this to end."

"Me either."

"Luckily we have somewhere else to go."

"And here I thought this was the end of the night."

"Nope, I have a few more things up my sleeve. Let's go."

After returning our skates we ran across the street to this hotel. O'rion sensed me tense up and reassured me we weren't here for nothing like that. Once inside O'rion stepped away to talk to someone while I admired the décor. The hotel lobby was decorated silver, red, and pink. There were pink and red hearts everywhere with Roses and candles lined up on the floor leading up to the elevator. Orion came back and escorted me to the elevator. As we rode the elevator my anxiety began to kick in. I couldn't imagine what other surprises he had in store. When the doors open I was in awe. ON top of the hotel was glass igloos. Each igloo had a fireplace, two chairs, a small table, and blankets. The hostess took his name and led us to our private igloos. Words couldn't begin to describe how I was feeling right now. I had never seen anything so beautiful. Orion pulled out my chair and then sat down across from me. From my seat, I could see the ice skating rink we were just at.

"Wow, this is beautiful Ry."

"I know, when I saw this I just knew it would be a perfect way to end the night."

"It really is. Thank you again."

"Thanks for allowing me to take you out and show you everything you deserve."

"If you would have told me six months ago I would be here I wouldn't believe you. For years I've prayed and dreamt of having a new life. I gave up but you restored my faith and you kept your word. You told me you would help me and you've done that and then some."

"That day I met you Sparkle I knew something was special about you. You were so beautiful I was mad I never got your name. When I saw you again that day at the party even after all that transpired I knew you were going to be in my life one way or another. The way you made me feel that day was something I would never forget. It was something I never felt. Having you this close to me these past few weeks has been everything I knew it would be. I meant what I said earlier. I want you to be happy and I will do everything in my power to make you happy."

"I want to make you happy too," I confessed.

"You do more than you even realize."

Our waiter came shortly after and took our order. Everything on the menu looked so good I had a hard time decided. I ended up getting the steamed lobster tail, garlic mashed potatoes and asparagus. O'rion got the filet minion, baked potato, and broccoli. We both got the Cesar salads and we were sharing the crab cakes. Before I meals came they brought us a bucket of ice and a bottle of Champagne. We sipped slowly as we talked. I was feeling a light buzz or maybe I was so happy I was floating. Either way, I felt great. Once dinner arrived Ry moved his chair closer to me. The conversation flowed so effortlessly. We talked about everything under the sun. I never laughed so much in my life. As they cleared away our plates O'rion brought me over to the fireplace. We sat on the floor on top of blankets and pillows. Orion wrapped us in a blanket as I laid comfortably on him. Our waiter then brought us a tray of graham crackers, marshmallows and chocolate to make s'mores. We made our s'mores and then fed them to each other. Ry had chocolate on the side of his mouth. I wanted to do something out of my comfort zone so I leaned over and licked it off. Using my finger I wiped the rest of it away.

"Sorry I couldn't help myself."

"Don't be sorry I liked it. Don't be embarrassed or ashamed to do something. I'm yours Sparkle."

"And I'm yours." I blushed.

I didn't want the night to end but it was getting late. Today couldn't have gone any better. Ry and I held hands as we walked the streets of NYC. We barely talked but there was nothing left to be said. I was where I was supposed to be and that was with O'rion. By the time we got back to the apartment we showered and ate cake and ice cream on the couch until we fell asleep.

O'RION HAD ME UP EARLY THIS MORNING. I WAS SLEEPING SO peacefully in his arms. Even though we fell asleep on the couch I had never slept so damn good. Ry said he had one more surprise for me and at this point, I was overwhelmed with it all. In a good way though. Sitting on the balcony enjoying my coffee I waited for Ry to come and get me for my surprise. When the time finally came he blindfolded me before leading me inside.

"Do you trust me Sparkle?"He asked.

"Ye-yes." I stuttered.

"You don't sound too sure."

"Yes, I trust you O'rion. The blindfold just makes me nervous."

"Don't worry, I'm right here and we're not going far."

"Okay."

"Good now stand right here."

I felt when he left from my side. My heart was pounding. I heard the door open then close. Someone was standing in front of me. I could feel them and smell them. The smell was so familiar to me. It smelt like Curve in the blue bottle. I would never forget that smell, it was what my mom wore almost every day. That's when it hit me. This couldn't be real could it? Tears welled up in my eyes drenching the blindfold quickly.

"Ry." I cried out.

"Its okay baby." He said taking off my blindfold.

Opening my eyes the connected with a pair that matched mine. She was crying too. My mom was standing here right in front of me. She looked exactly how I remembered. Reaching out my hand I touched her face. I knew this was real but I still couldn't believe it.

"Mo-mom!"

"it's me baby, it's me."

Throwing myself into her arms she caught me as my legs gave out underneath me. Sitting on the floor with me we cried until we couldn't cry anymore. I've been waiting for this moment. A moment I never thought would happen. My mom picked me up off the floor and wiped my face.

"How? I don't understand."

"Your friend here found me and reached out to me last week."

"Ry thank you thank you so much," I said running to him.

"You're welcome, baby girl. I'm glad I could do this for you."

"How though? I mean ugh I can't believe this."

"Facebook. It took a little bit of research but I found her."

"I had given up, I thought I was never going to find you."

"I never gave up looking for you Sparkle. I looked you up on Facebook as soon as I got out. For the last year and a half, I've searched and searched but it seemed impossible."

"It was designed that way."

"What do you mean?"

"it's a long story."

"Well I got time and I would love to catch up with you if you want to that is."

"Of course I do. I've waited for this moment."

"How about I take you guys to the diner. I'll drop you guys off." O'Rion offered.

"Let me just get my purse and we can go."

Running into my room I grabbed my purse and ran back into the living room. My mom and O'rion were laughing and it made my heart sing. This view was picture perfect. Honestly, I still couldn't believe this was real.

"I'm ready."

"Let's go."

O'rion grabbed his keys and we left. I sat in the back with my mom so we could talk the whole way there. Every time I looked up at Ry, he was smiling from ear to ear. I didn't know how I could ever thank him for this but I would die trying. O'rion dropped us off at the diner a few blocks from the apartment. He slipped me some money to pay for the food and left. I tried to protest but he said this was all him. The diner was empty when we walked in. We were seated immediately in a booth near the window.

"I'm sorry Sparkle. I never wanted to leave you. I tried to take a plea, I tried everything I could to get back to you." She cried.

"Don't cry ma. You're here now. That's all that matters to me. We have nothing but time to get to know each other."

"I know I can't help it. You've grown into a beautiful young lady. My baby girl is a woman now."

"You should have seen me a few months ago. I wasn't always this put together."

"Tell me everything. I know I've missed so much."

"Well, dad married Angela."

"Angela? Angela Williams?"

"Yup."

"That bitch always wanted your father."

"So you knew that?"

"Yea that's why I started to stay away. She was messy and used to do little slick shit like I didn't or wouldn't notice. "

"Wow! I'm not surprised though. She's still messy and a bitch so nothing's changed."

"Really? The bitch still at it? "

"She made my life miserable, I actually ran away not too long ago."

"WHAT!" she shrieked.

"Yea at twenty years old I was nothing. Nothing to them at all just there maid. What's worse is I was nothing to myself. For years I just let them do whatever they wanted to me. I didn't know how to stand up to them. I didn't know how to stand up for myself. It wasn't until I met O'rion that I did something about it. "

"From our conversation, I can tell he's a stand-up guy."

"He's amazing. He would send me daily affirmations and speak life into me. I didn't know I needed it until I received it. In this short amount of time, he's come into my life and showed me what happiness was like. I couldn't have asked for someone better."

"That's great we can talk about that later though. I need to know about miss Angela."

Before I could catch her up our waiter came and took our order. As we sipped our drinks I told her everything from the beginning. From moving to Brooklyn to him marrying Angela. I told her about the abuse and the mistreatment I endured for all the years. We both cried but for different reasons. I cried because I was happy to be free, she was crying because of guilt. I didn't want her to feel guilty. There was no time for that. I wasn't mad at her, not even a little bit. I was glad she was back in my life. I had my mother. My life was complete.

"Sparkle I am so sorry you had to deal with that. This is not what I wanted for you. Never in a million years. "

"I know mom I'm not mad or anything. "

"I'll spend forever making it up to you."

"Just don't leave me again."

"I won't. I promise. But I do have a favor to ask?"

"Anything."

"Whats the bitch address? I wanna put hands and feet on that ass. And wait until I see your damn father."

"I would but I don't want to lose you again."

"I understand but if I see her ass in the streets I'm not saying I won't knock her ass out." She smiled.

"That's fine with me." I laughed.

"I'm sure you have questions for me also. Don't be afraid to ask."

"What happened? I want to know everything. I mean one day you were there and the next you weren't.."

"When I was in my mid-twenties I was diagnosed with bipolar disorder. By that time I was married to your father. Your father was beginning to resent me. My behavior and my mood were all over. We couldn't understand what it was. So he made me go to the doctor or he was going to leave. I was diagnosed with Bi-polar disorder and that's when shit really hit the roof. It took him forever to come around. He wanted me to pray it away. He didn't believe In all of that medication shit."

"What did you do? I read some of your diary so I knew that part but I never finished."

" I had to try something to save my marriage. I started secretly taking medication to help. I hid it from everyone up until my accident. That's when it all came out."

"It all makes sense now," I mumbled.

"What makes sense?"

"Why dad never wanted to talk about you."

"Your father was not only ashamed of me but he was hurt I hid it from him for all that time. The moment I realized I might not see you again or talk to you again was one of the worst days of my life. I e=never meant to hurt anybody. I just wanted a different medication. I never had bad side effects before. I thought I could handle it but I fell asleep behind the wheel and killed somebody. There was a child in the car and they were injured but they lived. "

"Wow."

"I fought hard to get that child endangerment charge dismissed. I wanted to get back to you as soon as possible. I knew I would have to do some time but not 10 years. All these years my only wish was that you knew I didn't leave you on purpose."

"In my heart, I knew even though I didn't know anything about what happened until a few months ago I just knew. Unfortunate things happened to both of us but we're here now. "

"We're here now." She said as she held my hands.

We sat there and caught up for almost two hours. Jail had hardened her. I could tell but she was still how I remembered. Sweet as hell but sour when she wanted to be. Two hours wasn't long enough but this was a new start for both of us. After paying the bill we stepped outside to wait for Ry. I didn't want to leave her, I felt like I would never see her again but she reassured me that wouldn't happen. When we got to her place I walked her to the door.

"I'll see you soon Sparkle. Today was amazing but it wasn't long enough."

"It sure wasn't but this was the best day ever."

"Before I go I have something for you. You only turn twenty-one once."

Opening her purse she pulled out a long velvet box. When I opened the box a gold locket shined in the sunlight. Opening it up it was a picture of my and my mom when I was a baby.

"This is beautiful. Thank you."

"You're welcome, baby girl."

After helping me put it on we hugged for what felt like hours but was only a few minutes. We both had tears in our eyes as we stood there staring at each other. I didn't want this moment to end.

"Why are you crying?" I asked.

"Because I'm back with my baby girl. Why are you crying? "She chuckled.

"I don't want to leave you."

"Then don't."

"What do you mean?"

"If you want I have enough room here. You could come stay with me. We can get to know each other and make up for lost time."

"Wow, I don't know what to say."

"Just think about it, the offer is always on the table."

"Yea I just need some time to process this all."

"I know its' a lot but trust me its no pressure at all. Don't keep O'rion waiting we'll talk later."

"Okay, mom ill call you."

"Please do."

We said our goodbyes and O'rion and I headed home. My head was spinning. Move-in with her? Was it too soon? Would it work? What if we didn't like each other? She lived close by I could always visit right? So many thoughts ran through my head but all I could really think about was O'rion. The whole ride home was quiet. I was having an internal battle with myself. Do I stay with Ry and see where this goes or do I reconnect with my mom. They were the only people I had I didn't want to ruin my relationships with either of them.

"Sparkle why are you crying?"

"Huh? Crying?" Touching my face I felt the cold tears that stained my face.

"Yes your crying. Are you ok?."

"Honestly no, my mind is just all over and I feel like I'm suffocating."

"Breath, we'll be home soon."

Ry rubbed my hand trying to soothe me as he parked the car. He came around and opened my door and picked me up. Ry carried me the whole way to the apartment as I cried into his neck. Once he opened the door he placed me on the couch and disappeared to the back. Crawling into the fetal position I laid there trying to calm my breathing. O'rion came back shortly after and brought me to the bathroom where he prepared me a bath. Even though it was daytime he lit some candles and had soft music playing in the background.

"Relax for a bit and then we'll talk ok?"

Nodding my head Ry kissed me on the forehead before closing the door behind him. Stripping out of my clothes I slipped into the steamy water. It was the perfect temperature. Closing my eyes I leaned my head back and tried to relax. The sound of Erykah Badu had me so relaxed I was drifting off to sleep. Once the water got cold I drained the tub and took a quick shower before getting out and getting dressed. O'rion was on the couch watching TV when I emerged. When he saw me he turned the Tv off and motioned for me to come. As I sat Ry pulled me closer to him and just held me. IT was quiet for a few moments as I tried to get my thoughts together.

"You ready to talk now?"

"Yes." I said sitting up." I don't even know where to begin."

"Did your mom say something to you?"

"She did but nothing that should upset me. She um asked me to move in with her."

"Sparkle that's great. Why are you crying then?"

"I don't know what to do. I have my mom back and I would love to go and live with her and get to know her."

"So what's the problem then?'

"I don't want to lose you."

"Aww Sparkle. Look at me. I'm not going anywhere. I told you it was me and you and I meant that. I knew there was a possibility this could happen but I didn't let that stop me from reconnecting you with your mom. I wanted this for you because seeing you happy is everything to me. Seeing that beautiful smile on your face is what keeps me going. If you want to go live with your mom that's fine."

"Really?"

"Of course. I know this whole situation isn't ideal but we're making the best of it. I enjoy having you here with me. I love knowing that in the next room you're there and you're safe. That's all that matters to me. So what if we won't be living together you can always come and visit or spend the night whatever you want. Long as you don't plan on leaving my life I can deal with you living fifteen minutes away. Or you can split your time if that makes you feel better. Spend some days with me here and some days with your mom."

"You know what I really like that idea. That's what I'm going to do. I was so scared that you would be upset I almost gave myself a panic attack." I nervously laughed.

"Never in a million years."

"I still don't know what I want to do though. I mean it sounds so tempting but correct me if I'm wrong I feel like we're building something and I kind of want to see where that takes us."

"You're correct. We are building something. Like I said this isn't the ideal situation. Usually, you date for a while then move it. We moved right on in. It's nothing wrong with doing things a little backward but its what you feel comfortable with. The only thing I ever wanted for you Sparkle was to be safe, happy, and loved. You have all of that now."

"And it's all because of you. I don't know how ill ever repay you for what you've done for me. You give me life, you give me purpose. You make me feel things I've only ever dreamed and read about. I believe you were sent to me for a reason. I thought meeting you was the best day of my life. Then I thought being free was the best day of my life but nope. My birthday was the best day of my life. You've given me a day to remember and a lifetime to forget.

Sparkle

If you would have told me I would be sitting in Paris outside the Eiffel tower with the love of my life I would laugh in your face. After all the shit I've been through in my life I made it out on top. After years of being unloved, I'm loved and it's the best feeling in the world. My self-esteem was no longer low, I no longer felt like a burden. For once in my life I had friends. I came and went as I pleased. I had money in my pockets that I earned. Going to school to become a CNA was one of the best things I could have done. It made me step outside my comfort zone and find out who I was. It took me a while to figure out what field I wanted to go in. I liked helping and taking care of people. This time though I was doing it under my own terms.

Although I no longer had a relationship with my father I had one with my mom. We were like best friends from the day we reconnected. Splitting my time between her and Ry turned out to be the best for all three of us. After eight months though I moved back with O'rion to deepen our bond. My mother and I talked every day and saw each other every Sunday. I wouldn't lie and say

I didn't want a relationship with my father. Every girl does. I'm not ready to accept an apology and the fact that he's still with she who shall not be named made it harder too. I was happy and content with my little family and my life. I had an amazing boyfriend, a loving mom, and some friends. I couldn't ask for anything better.

"What you thinking about babe?" O'rion asked.

"Just how grateful I am to be here with you." I smiled.

"I'm glad to be here with you too. Isn't this beautiful?"

"It is. We've done so much this year but this tops it."

"I know. You know I love you right?"

"Yes I know my love, you tell me and show me every day."

"Cuz I want you to know how I feel about you. When I met you over two years ago I never thought we would be here. Sitting outside the Eiffel tower at sunset. I knew you were special the day I met you I just didn't know you would change my life the way you did. thank you for loving me and caring about me the way that you do. The little notes you leave on my breakfast to the way you sing for me as we lay in bed. I cherish all of those moments-"

"Baby." I interrupted.

"Let me finish. "He smiled," I say all that to say that every day with you is better than the last. And I want to continue making these memories. I want to continue to grow. I want to grow old with you. What I'm saying is Will you Marry me Sparkle?"

O'rion pulled out a small Dark red box and got on his knees. The tears I had been holding in flowed freely. My words caught in my throat I looked around to see if anybody else was seeing this. Was this really happening? Looking into his eyes I knew this was the man for me. The way he loved me and cared for me no other man could do. No matter how little time has passed I wanted to be his wife. When you knew you knew.

"YES! YES!YES" I cried.

The people around us cheered and congratulated us as O'rion

slipped the diamond ring on my finger. Picking me up off the ground he kissed me like he's never kissed me before. There was always love behind his kisses but this one was deeper than that. I felt it deep in my soul.

"I love you so much Sparkle."

"I love you too," I replied wiping a lone tear away from his face.

THE SILHOUETTE OF OUR LOVEMAKING BOUNCED OFF THE walls of our candlelit room. The view of the Eiffel Tower from our balcony shined bright in the background making this moment even more spectacular. O'rion stared deep into my soul as he slowly stroked my insides. Tears stained my face once again as another orgasm erupted. He placed tender kisses from my forehead down to the crease of my neck. Wrapping my legs around his back allowed him to go exploring deeper into my honey pot.

"Oooohh Ry." I moaned.

"Look at me." He demanding through clenched teeth.

Our eyes connected and our bodies erupted like a volcano. Sweat rolled down our bodies making us stick together but there was no place id rather be right now. Ry kissed me again as he released his essence inside of me. When he was done he rolled over and pulled me close to him. Laying my head on his chest listened to his heartbeat as I caught my breath. His seemed to match mine perfectly. The cool breeze coming from the open balcony tickled my skin giving me good bumps. Seemingly heightening my senses.

"How do you feel?'

"Like I'm floating in the clouds above the earth," I replied.

"Good soon to be Mrs. Miller."

"That sounds so damn good." I giggled.

"It does, doesn't it? What type of wedding would you want?"

"I don't know something small long as we have a nice ass honeymoon I don't care. Do you want a short engagement or a long one?"

"At least a year. No more than two. I want to travel some more and enjoy you before jumping into wedding planning. Maybe find a new place to move. Whatever we decide to do as long as it's with you I'm content. As long as you're happy I'm happy."

"I can agree with that."

As the conversation faded off and the reality of it all began to settle in. I began to dream of my life as his wife. I could see it all so clearly. No matter what happened in my life this moment was worth going through everything. Because if I hadn't I would have never met O'rion.

"Thank you for allowing me to love you Sparkle."

"Thank you for wanting to love me."

THE END!

For updates follow me on Facebook Olexa Renee
On Instagram @ author_jrenee
Or join my readers group Beyond Ordinary
Books